Every Little Thing

Anna Maloney

EVERY LITTLE THING
An 18thWall Productions book published by
arrangement with Anna Maloney
verba mea in minibus
desiderium meum
Cover by Viviane Rivas
Design by Adventures on Earth Productions
Text Copyright
Every Little Thing © Anna Maloney

ISBN-13: 978-1-946033-08-6
ISBN-10: 1-946033-08-1

PUBLISHERS NOTE
This is a work of fiction. Names, characters, places, and incidents either are the products of
the author's imagination or used fictitiously. Any resemblance to actual persons, living or
dead, business establishments, events, locales, public figures, private figures, and fictional
characters is entirely coincidental.

To my family, my squad, and my fake siblings,
James and Nikki, who encouraged me
to start this all in the first place

Acknowledgements

It is so often that I try to stand alone that sometimes it is suprising to turn and see how many people stand with me.

My parents, my twin brother, Sean, and my whole family have always encouraged me to follow my interest in writing, and I thank them for that—but it's James and Nikki who gave me the opportunity to do it not as a hobby, but as a real job. Without them I don't know if I ever would have published a novel, and if I had, certainly not so early.

Capucine, Aidan, and Ryan—you're my best friends, and you gave me all the encouragement I could ever need while I was in the process of writing this. Telling you about how it was going was always a highlight in my days. Thank you so much for being my friends, and for supporting me.

All my Lovin,

AM

Table of Contents

Chapter 1

Eyes flitted open in the dark. There was a quiet groan as a hand slowly moved to check if someone was still beside it—they were, and the hand patted the sleeping form. As always, Lois McCarthy woke up at 5:00 AM, no longer needing an alarm. Slowly rising out of bed, Lois turned and put her slippers on, got up, reached over for her robe, and silently padded into the master bedroom's attached bathroom. Without even needing to think, Lois followed her routine: shower, shave, get dressed, do hair, do makeup. She was done by 5:40, the ten minutes extra from this being a hair washing day.

Lois silently left the bathroom and glanced over at her husband, Paul. He didn't need to wake up until 7:30, so she left the room. Her kids needed to be up by 6:30 for school, so Lois headed downstairs and started on breakfast. As everything heated up, Lois gathered up any spare school supplies her two daughters had left scattered around the house, packing their bags up and putting them in the designated chairs.

Breakfast was scrambled eggs, toast, bacon, ham, fried apple rings, and pineapple juice. Lois knew she was right on schedule when she heard the pattering of feet just as she began putting food on plates. She'd been sure to leave enough to cook when it was time for Paul to wake up, smiling as Mary came down the stairs.

"Morning, mommy!" Mary called, smiling.

"Good morning, sweetheart," Lois said on instinct, bending over and kissing Mary on the cheek. Her older sister Linda followed down shortly, yawning and quiet.

"Good morning, sweetheart," She repeated, pulling Linda into a sleepy hug as Mary sat down for breakfast. The child waited patiently for Lois and Linda to sit down; she knew that they were on a schedule, though it wasn't conscious for her yet. She was only seven, and such things were less her concern. Linda, at nine, was much more aware of it, but she didn't feel the pressure the way Lois did. Lois ran on a clock, constantly chasing after the impossible prospect of somehow getting ahead of schedule.

Mary and Linda began eating as Lois slowly munched on some spare eggs. Paul liked to eat with her, but so did the kids, so she ate a little with them and had her full breakfast with her husband.

"What's school going to be like today?" she asked pleasantly. Mary, as always, answered first.

"Today we're going to be doing multiplication and division, and we're going to do something with newspapers. She said we get to cut them up and put them on a collage."

Lois smiled. Mary was good at math, and as much as the teacher encouraged Lois to push her daughter in a more 'female friendly' direction, Lois was determined to feed Mary's interest.

"Do I get to see your collage when you're done?"

Mary nodded, then paused. "I have to turn it in, but when we get it back I'll bring it to you," the child promised, and Lois nodded with a grin that made Mary smile. Much of Mary's—and Linda's—work hung on the walls and fridge.

"How about you, Linda?" Lois asked, turning to her older daughter. Linda looked at her with bleary eyes.

"We're reading through a few books and comparing them. And we're peer editing our short stories today."

Lois gave her daughter a grin and Linda smiled a little. She was still too tired to be up for much conversation, but Linda had always been good at writing.

"Oh, good, honey! I'm sure everyone will love it."

Linda nodded and turned her focus back to her food just as Mary finished eating. Lois got up and swept up her and Mary's dishes, putting them into the sink and pulling on rubber gloves to wash them without ruining her manicure.

"Mary, get your school clothes on, make your bed, and get ready for school, darling. Linda, just give me your plate when you're finished and do the same." The children replied with a unanimous 'yes, mama,' used to this.

Lois waited with Mary and Linda on their porch for the carpool that came to pick them up and bring them to the elementary school, over in the town next to the suburban development. While this wasn't one of Levitt's Levittowns, it had been built with the same idea in mind: every house looked almost identical, the only changes being colour and if they mirrored the one next to them or were exact structural copies. Lois's lawn was recognisable by her well-manicured garden with agreed-upon flowers, which she'd mapped out with the homeowner's association.

As they sat on the porch of the mint green house, Lois could see several of her neighbors doing the same. Lois waved at Nancy and Cynthia, who were out with their kids and used the same carpool that Patricia's husband Harold drove. Something else flashed in the corner of her eye, perhaps another person waving, but when Lois turned she didn't see anything.

It wasn't long before Harold's station wagon pulled up, right on time. Mary and Linda gave Lois last kisses and took the paper bags with their lunches from her before running over to climb in. Lois stood on the steps and waved as they drove away. She waited until they were out of sight before fetching the newspaper to put on the table and going back into the house at 7:25, heading up to the master bedroom.

Going through the dark, Lois bent down next to Paul's half of the bed where he was still sleeping.

"Honey," she whispered, before saying a bit louder with a hand on his shoulder, "Paul. It's time to wake up." In the dark room, she could see him open his eyes, looking at her with a soft smile.

"Morning," he mumbled. Lois smiled as he pulled her over into a sleepy hug. Hc kissed her on the cheek as she wrapped her arms around him, chuckling quietly.

Lois had always felt lucky that she and her husband got along so well; most of her friends didn't actually love their husbands. She didn't talk about it, as it was rude and bad show, but she knew it and they knew it. If she really thought about it, Patricia and Harold, along with Nancy and James, really seemed like the only ones who loved each other, and even they didn't seem to get along as well as Lois and Paul did. Cynthia and Winston were more like good friends, and the others were trapped in more or less loveless marriages. It hadn't escaped Lois's notice that they had all gotten together in high school, whereas she had met her husband later on like Patricia and Nancy.

Once it was 7:30, the alarm next to them went off and Paul's hand slapped onto the off button on instinct, groaning a little.

"We need to sleep in more," he murmured as Lois got up, heading into the open bathroom to fix her hair back up.

"I'd love to, but you know how it is."

Paul got out of bed, stretching before following her, his arms wrapping around her from behind as he bent over to put his head on her shoulder.

"Ah, yes. The schedule."

Lois nodded and he turned and kissed her cheek, eliciting a smile as she put her hands over his.

"This weekend?"

Lois paused.

"But the store."

Lois edited gossip and makeup columns for the local newspaper, but their primary source of income was Paul's general store in town.

"Just Sunday, love."

She paused before slowly nodding. Paul gave her a wide grin, turning her so he could kiss her proper this time. Lois smiled into it, and as he pulled back she reached forward and wiped the lipstick he'd rubbed off from his lips.

"It's your colour," she joked, and he laughed as he turned to get ready to shower. Lois turned to the mirror and reapplied her lipstick from the tube in the cabinet behind it before heading back downstairs to cook his breakfast.

Lois was putting the plates on the table as he came downstairs, wearing a pair of dark gray slacks and a tucked in plaid button up without a tie. It was very casual compared to what most of the husbands—aside from Harold, who was a mechanic—wore, but Paul insisted that it made people more at ease in the shop, finding him friendlier. He sat down next to her, grinning at breakfast and taking the newspaper as she put down a mug of coffee in front of him.

"I see it's Monday," he observed before beginning to eat. Lois nodded. With every day being more or less the same, her husband had some trouble remembering what day it was sometimes. His wife's rigid agenda—like the daily change in menu—helped clue him in before he opened the newspaper. Lois always knew, but it was because she made a point to know—if she didn't check the papers and keep mind of it, her days blended together too.

Paul scanned the paper quickly before folding it back up and putting it to the side. He always left the paper for Lois, as he could read one at the store between customers.

"How were Linda and Mary?" He asked as Lois slowly ate.

"Mary is excited for a project at school. Linda's too tired in the mornings to tell, but they're checking their stories today, and hers is quite good. I think she'll be happy."

Paul nodded with a wistful smile, staring for a few moments as his wife looked down at her food. Paul didn't have the chance to spend a lot of time with his children during the week, though occasionally Linda would come visit him at the store after school.

"What are you up to today?"

Paul reached forwards and took one of her hands, intertwining his fingers with hers as she looked up at him.

"Oh, we have knitting club today," she said with a smile, and he nodded.

"That's good. Are you almost done with those next blankets?"

Lois was quick with her fingers, so they'd decided to sell some of her blankets at the general store to try and get some extra cash.

"I've gotten about fifteen of them done, darling."

He could tell she was a bit melancholy, which was another part of why he wanted to have her sleep in more. Paul and Lois had moved from the city to Rose Park five years ago, and since then their lives had taken up such an endless repetition that Paul felt stagnant. That was nothing compared to what had happened to Lois, however, who seemed to have become so controlled by their schedule that she had to be convinced to take a night out. She'd become more rigid and more withdrawn—scarcely resembling her spirited younger self.

Paul had talked with the other husbands, and while most of them seemed to like their wives being so sedated and dedicated to this monotony, Harold had understood. Harold's wife, Patricia, was a very artsy type who had felt stifled until she joined Cynthia's knitting club. Paul's brother, James, had a similar opinion, telling him that Nancy had been happier after joining the knitting club as well. Paul had immediately gone and convinced Lois to join, and while the company had seemed to cheer her, Paul still made an effort to try and give her variety.

"You said that Barbara joined?" He asked, trying to remember anything she'd told him about the club in the past. She never really talked about it.

"Yes. It's Cynthia, Nancy, Patricia, Eleanor, Barbara, and I." Somewhat small, but comfortable. The neighborhood wasn't even half full, so it was plentiful for the options available.

Paul nodded and watched as Lois got up and took his plate, which he looked down at just in time to realise he'd emptied it. She put all the dishes in the sink and pulled on her gloves to start washing them.

He glanced at his watch to see that it was 8:00, which meant that he had to leave in the next fifteen minutes in order to open the store at 8:30. Lois had an innate sense of the schedule that both impressed and unnerved Paul. Before he could say anything, Lois turned to him.

"You should get everything you need together, dear."

Paul finished his coffee before getting his coat, his keys, and his shoes. He didn't need anything else that wasn't already in his pockets, so Lois was practically dragging him to his car by 8:10.

"You don't want to be late," she insisted as they walked through the house to their garage, a paper bag with his lunch in her hands. The two car garage held their car, tools, and other supplies that didn't have a place in the house but needed to be easily accessible, including another refrigerator and a large freezer.

"I'll be there with more than enough time," he countered as he paused outside the car, put off by her antsiness at him possibly breaking schedule; her hands were fidgeting and she nervously gestured for him to get in.

"Lois. There's plenty of time," he assured her, but she wasn't convinced. Paul opened the door and put his lunch in before leaning over and kissing her, slightly reluctant as he got in their car and drove off for the store.

Now that everyone else was out of the house, the daily cleaning routine began. Lois cleaned the bathrooms before making her bed, putting in a load of laundry, going to the kitchen to clean out the coffeemaker, and mopping the linoleum floors. As it was a Monday, Lois went through the weekly tasks of scrubbing the oven clean, going through the refrigerator to throw out old food and clean it up, and finally doing the same with the cupboards. She then swept up the rest of the rooms, dusting and taking the rugs out to beat the dirt out of them.

Once she'd replaced the rugs, it was time to put the laundry in the dryer and load the washer with the second load. Lois gathered all the clothing that couldn't be run through a dryer and took it to the back porch, going past it into the yard to hang the clothing up on her clothing lines. She knew she was on time because she could see other lines being filled with clothing just over the fences that separated backyards.

Lois then proceeded to hunt the house for spare articles of clothing that needed to be washed, gathering them in a hamper to be put in the final laundry load. After that, she went back and opened the windows to air out the rooms, took out the garbage, and put anything out of place where it belonged.

15

That was it for Mondays, and it took her a good few hours—
Lois was done with everything by 11:30, at which point she
began her daily exercise regimen. Lois made sure to dedicate
at least half an hour to this every day, turning on the radio to
listen as she did stretches and simple exercises. At 12, Lois
changed into gardening clothes and headed outside.

In the backyard, Lois maintained several flowered plots
and a small garden with herbs, spices, and simple foodstuff
that they used often like potatoes, tomatoes, peas, lima beans,
onions, and carrots. Lois, at 30 despite appearances of youth,
had lived with parents who hammered home the concept of
growing your own food out of necessity. Even now, when
Paul's store offered them enough money and food to live very
comfortably, she couldn't let it go.

Chapter 2

Lois spent the next two hours in one of her favourite places, picking weeds and tending to her plants. She only stopped when her internal clock warned her of the imminent arrival of her children—she got changed and cleaned up just in time for Mary and Linda to come walking up the sidewalk at 3:45. Her nieces, Maureen and Jane, were walking with them,

"Hello Linda, hello Mary," Lois greeted them with a grin and kisses as she met them at the sidewalk.

"Hello Maureen, hello Jane. Tell your mother hello for me."

She gave her nieces a hug and a kiss each, watching them walk to Nancy and James's house next door before taking both of her children by the hand. They slowly walked up the porch and into the house, Mary swinging her arms as Linda yawned.

"How was school today?"

"We started our collages! I found a picture of someone who looked just like you, mama!"

"I got an A on my story."

Lois congratulated both of them, turning with more attention to Linda.

"Oh, that's great, honey! Did everyone like it?"

Linda nodded with a summery smile, and Lois grinned.

"I'm so proud of you. You're such a great writer."

Linda turned to the ground, embarrassed but grinning.

Lois prepared them a snack as they—well, as Mary talked more about what they'd done. She deftly cut an apple into chunks, cutting the skins off of Linda's. She then smeared some peanut butter on them before serving them on two plates, sitting across from her children as they ate. There were oatmeal cookies cooking in the oven, but those were for the knitting club and the kids knew it.

"And we went through all these magazines, and there's a lot about fashion, but I just cut out everything purple 'cos we're supposed to do a theme, and I chose a colour theme, so I chose purple, 'cos that's the best colour. The lady that looks like you is wearing a purple dress, mama! It's real pretty. And then we cut out letters from headlines to make our own false headlines, and they're supposed to catch your eye, so mine is about purple becoming the national colour of America!" Mary beamed. She'd babbled this all very excitedly, only pausing to take and swallow bites of food.

"Well, that sounds wonderful, Mary. Perhaps when you are a scientist, you can write about how purple makes people happier, or how it's the best wavelength." Lois herself had been quite keen on science as a child—which was a big part of why she was determined to let Mary follow this passion—but her knowledge was not very extensive.

"Yeah, mama!" Mary agreed. Lois turned to Linda, who had been perfectly happy to let Mary ramble on and on. Mary was much more outgoing than Linda had ever been. Linda was quiet and speculative, much more interested in being a writer and perhaps a journalist. Lois was even saving up to get her older daughter a fancy camera.

"So, tell me about your story, Linda."

Linda, voice sweet and quiet like her mother's, explained how her story had been about an alien coming to a neighborhood and trying to fit in, finding it easy due to the fact that everyone acted the same and worked on a schedule.

"Very creative, Linda. That's a great idea for a story," Lois said with a grin, surmising that this must have been a creative fiction prompt. Linda smiled and went back to focusing on her apple halves as Mary finished and jumped up.

"I'm going to go draw!" she announced before running out of the room, and Lois got up and began to wash the dishes.

"Linda, do you have any plans for today?" Lois asked, glancing back to see Linda shake her head.

"Would you mind going down to the store to see your father? He likes to spend time with you, and you can write while you're there. It'll be quieter there than here." As if on cue, a rock record began sounding through the house.

"Sure, mom."

Linda got up and brought her dish over to Lois before leaving the kitchen to get ready to leave.

Lois wandered over to where Linda was pulling on her shoes and organising what she'd take to the store after the dishes were done.

"Linda," She started, pausing slightly, "Could you tell your father that I love him, and give him this?" She held out a little paper bag.

"Of course, mom."

Lois gave her a kiss on the cheek and a hug before walking out onto the porch with her and watching her bike off in the direction of the store, only sitting down when she was out of sight. While she was there Harold came walking up the street, waving before coming over up onto the porch. Lois jumped to her feet.

Harold and Paul had become very good friends after taking the car to his garage, and from that, Lois had become friends with him as well.

"Hello, Harry. Shouldn't you be at the shop?"

Harold was wearing his jumpsuit and a jean jacket; judging by how messy they were, it was apparent he'd been there sometime that day.

"I'm on break. I'll be going back soon. I just wanted to stop by to talk."

Lois nodded and they sat down on the porch, Harold tactfully choosing a chair without a cushion.

"I got the part, for the next time you bring the car in. I can show Paul how to keep it up, too. Just to let you know. But, uh, Patricia saw Cynthia today, and I overheard them talking about something that had to do with a case Winston has."

Lois was clearly interested, leaning in a bit.

"Oh?"

"Yeah, you not hear about it?"

"No, I haven't seen Cynthia since the last knitting club meeting."

Harold nodded, thoughtfully rubbing his short beard.

"Alright. Just wondering. Also, could you help me out in the garden real quick, before I go back to the shop?" Patricia wasn't a gardener by any means, so Lois wasn't at all surprised that he was coming to her.

"Sure. Let me just tell Mary."

With Mary in tow, they went with Harold down a few houses, just past where Lois's was visible. Harold and Patricia's house was light purple—something Mary quite enjoyed—and identical structurally to Lois and Paul's. Harold led them around the side of the house to the back where they kept a large flower garden. This was entirely Harold's garden, and Lois had learned quickly that he spent a lot of his time in it, similarly to her.

"I've been having trouble here with the azaleas."

He gestured to a few flowered bushes on the edge of the garden. They were drooping and had fewer flowers than more healthy bushes. The plant seemed dry but had obviously been watered recently.

"Oh, you need more mulch on those," she explained, and Harold snapped his fingers.

"Right. Yes."

At this point, Daniel had come out of the house. Very like Harold, the quiet eight year old was silently curious of the activities in the backyard. Seeing his dad, he ran over and gave him a hug.

"Daniel! Did you pass your test?" he asked, and Daniel nodded.

"I'm very proud of you."

"Hello, Danny!" Mary greeted him, and before Lois or Harold could say anything she was leading Daniel over to the back porch to colour with her.

Lois and Harold worked on his garden together for about a half hour, until the now rather muddy mechanic explained that he had to go back to the shop. Lois, Daniel, and Mary walked out to the front yard with him and waved as he drove off, at which point Patricia came out of the house.

"Oh, Lois! Did you help Harold with the azaleas?" she

asked, and Lois nodded, walking over to the front porch.

"Yes, they just need some mulch," Lois explained, and Patricia nodded.

"Listen, I—" she began, but paused.

"—can't wait to see you at knitting club tonight!" She looked pointedly at Mary and Daniel, who were muttering something amongst themselves.

"Yes, I'll see you tonight. It's at Cynthia's tonight, right?" Lois asked in an almost overly polite voice; the rotating schedule of homes for the knitting club was common knowledge amoungst members.

"Yes." Patricia kept up the pleasantries with a smile for the sake of the kids.

"Well, I'll see you then, I should get back home to start dinner. Goodbye, Daniel." Lois departed with a smile, Mary waving as her mother led her away by the hand. They were quiet as they walked back home, and Mary ran into the house to keep drawing as Lois went to the kitchen. She'd prepared some ham aspic the day before, so she started working on side dishes of canned tomato soup and buttered pan—fried vegetables using carrots, onions, and lima beans from her garden. The tomato soup simply needed to be heated, so she set it to simmer on the stove before cooking the vegetables and turning the heat way down to keep them warm.

She'd just set them to stay heated when she heard the car drive in, right on time—5:15.

"Hello, mom!" Linda greeted before going into the living room where Mary was colouring.

"Hello, dear!" Lois called out, stirring the vegetable as she felt two arms wrap around her, careful not to disturb her cooking.

"Hello, my love," Lois greeted, turning to see Paul's grinning face. He kissed her before settling his head on her shoulder, watching her turn the heat up so the soup and vegetables would be at a better serving temperature.

"Hello, my darling. Thank you for sending Linda down. And thank you for the package." He kissed her cheek again before letting go and taking the plates and utensils out, setting the table. She turned to see he was wearing what she'd sent in his hair, tucked behind his ear—a particularly bright blue Morning Glory flower.

Dinner was served at 5:30, as it always was on the nights that Lois had knitting club. The kids were at their seats already as Lois put down the ham aspic, Paul pulling out her chair for her as she sat before settling down himself.

"It looks delicious, dear."

Paul grinned as he served her, the kids, and then himself. The rest of dinner was a drone of conversation, the girls repeating what they'd already told Lois to Paul as she pretended to really be paying attention. She was listening enough to respond, but her mind was clearly somewhere else. None of her family noticed.

"Lois?"

The voice brought her out of a deep thought, and she blinked as she realised that Paul was staring at her. Mary and Linda had excused themselves, leaving her alone with him. He looked concerned.

"Oh, yes?"

He reached over and put his hands over hers, intertwining their fingers. The look hadn't left his face.

"You looked a bit spaced out. Were you thinking about something?"

She nodded, shaking her head slightly before giving him a reassuring smile.

"Oh, sorry, honey. I was thinking about what I have to do tomorrow."

Paul gave a sigh. He pulled his chair closer until he was right next to her, one of his hands leaving hers as he raised it up to cup her cheek. She leaned into it slightly and he gave a weary smile.

"Darling. You worry too much. We're supposed to be living."

"I am!" She insisted, but her expression contradicted her tone. She bit her lip and didn't meet his eye as his thumb gently stroked her cheek.

"Lois," he murmured, and she sighed. A few moments of

silence.

"You're right," she admitted in a whisper, and Paul drew her into a hug. She wrapped her arms around him tightly and closed her eyes.

"I know, I know."

He kissed her cheek as he readjusted, and she gave an 'Oh!' and a little chuckle as he pushed his chair back and pulled her onto his lap. With Lois's head cradled against his chest and shoulder, Paul moved to rest his chin atop of it.

"You have to live in the present."

She nodded in response.

"Remember right after our honeymoon? We visited my parents for dinner. The whole evening all they cared about was getting to the next thing—while we were greeting each other, they were worried about cocktails. While we were having cocktails, they were worried about dinner. While we were having dinner, they were worrying about desert…but we were having a great time, because we were just having a dinner."

"It's different now that we're a family and we're taking care of a house."

Paul looked down and gently put his thumb to her chin, tilting her head to face him.

"Lois. The house being taken care of is important, but it's not as important as having time to enjoy yourself."

She stared at him for a few moments, almost as if she didn't get it. He was about to say something else when she finally nodded, leaning up and kissing him.

"You're right," she admitted, pulling back a bit sooner than Paul would have liked; she gave a ghost of a giggle upon seeing him still leaned forwards, eyes closed.

"Glad you agree," he murmured before leaning forwards and kissing her again.

Chapter 3

Lois was almost late to leave for the knitting club by the time she and Paul managed to pull away from each other. He put her coat on for her and gave her a kiss goodbye as she left, standing on the porch until she disappeared into Cynthia's house.

"Lois! Hello, hello. Good evening." Cynthia greeted her at the door, giving her a quick hug and taking the tin of cookies and her knitting bag from her so she could shed her coat.

"Lois is here!" she exclaimed, calling over her shoulder. "It's already 6:27. You're not as early as usual."

"I was spending time with my husband," Lois replied with an audible smile as Patricia, Nancy, and Eleanor came out from the kitchen to greet her. Lois gave each of them a hug after she'd hung her coat on the rack and taken off her shoes, putting them next to everyone else's.

"Lois!"

"How are you?"

"You look happy. How were you spending that time?"

This last one was her sister-in-law Nancy, who laughed when Lois gave her a look.

"Just kidding, Lois. I know you're a good girl."

They had been hanging around in the kitchen as Cynthia heated up whatever they'd brought in the oven, but they migrated to the living room with all their sewing and knitting supplies now that only one person was missing.

"Where is Barbara?" Lois asked casually as she curled up on the end of the couch in her usual spot and started on a blanket for the shop. The other women weren't as focused on knitting, as was typical, but Lois felt a personal responsibility to her husband and his store.

"She told me she'd be a little late, she's stuck at home. She's having some problems with Richard."

Lois frowned; Richard was becoming a bit of a problem for Barbara. She'd never been very fond of him in the first place—despite his good humour and ability to go from joke to joke, she found him to be slightly off-putting.

"I know. I hope she gets here soon," Cynthia said once she saw Lois's expression, putting down freshly warmed angel food cake that Nancy had brought.

"So, Lois doesn't know about what Winston told you," Patricia blurted out, and everyone except Nancy turned to Lois with an excited, knowing look. Lois blinked.

"What's this?" Nancy asked, and all eyes went to her.

"You didn't hear either?"

"I didn't get the chance to tell her," Cynthia explained.

"Well, I feel a little better now. I'd hope you'd have told me if it's all this exciting," Lois said lightly, and Nancy chuckled.

"Go on, Cynthia," Eleanor encouraged.

"Well, let's wait for Barbara so I don't have to explain it twice. It's *very* interesting."

Lois had just managed to finish a blanket she'd left nearly done in her bag from the last meeting when they heard the front door open and quickly shut.

"Barbara?" several voices asked. Cynthia immediately rose to her feet and disappeared into the foyer. For a few moments their words were unintelligible, but before anyone could get up and see what was happening Barbara was led in. Her eyes were a bit red and wet but she was smiling.

"Hello! Sorry I'm late. I had to find someone to watch the kids."

Nancy looked like she was about to ask something, but Eleanor squeezed her arm and Nancy shut her mouth.

"Alright, everyone, here's what Winston told me," Cynthia started, before anyone's curiosity overrode their tact.

"For the past week I've heard this and that about some people claiming they've been robbed, or that their houses have been rifled through, even if nothing was stolen. Most of them weren't given too much thought because the boys at the precinct think they've just forgotten where they put something

25

when they find it somewhere other than they thought."

Cynthia gave a pause, at which point Patricia asked, "Were most of them housewives?" Cynthia nodded pointedly, smiling with satisfaction at her question.

"Yes. That's why they don't believe them. But I know there's something more to it, and Winston has realised it, too. They've been getting report after report, but after Winston talked with a nearby town's department, it's centralised here. Only Rose Park has been getting this rash of robbery and trespassing calls."

There was silence for a few seconds, before a cacophony of voices all spoke at once.

"One at a time, please!" Cynthia said a bit loudly.

Everyone tapered off, slightly surprised at the usually quiet woman.

"I see most of us are familiar with this. Barbara, how about you go first?"

Barbara nodded, putting down the ball of yarn she'd been having difficulty finding the end to. Lois tilted her head slightly—the end of the yarn was tucked in to the ribbon that Barbara had tied around the ball, easily visible.

"For the past week, we'd been losing silverware. Originally it was just one fork or one knife, but it picked up as time went on. At first I thought Jason or Leanne were just forgetting to put them back or taking them. I checked with Leanne first, since she's allowed to eat in her room, but we looked through it together and there wasn't any. So, I turned to my son. Jason's so little, I thought it must be him; they're bright and loud and he knows he's not supposed to use them except at meals. I asked him, but he's at that age, you know." Everyone nodded; Jason was five, and all the mothers had very clear memories of when their children were five.

"Anyway, I looked in all his regular hiding spots, and they weren't there. I even checked in the yard, but none of the grass was dug up, so I knew he hadn't been burying them. I asked Richard, but he said I must have just not checked everywhere." Her voice had gone a bit hard but quickly piped back up to the higher, faster pitch she'd been using.

26

"I went through the entire house, through every closet, anywhere they could be. I couldn't understand how they kept disappearing. I'm there all the time! Then I was worried someone might be stealing them, so I made a plan." There were a few light gasps; Barbara was usually fairly timid.

"You weren't going to try and outsmart a robber, were you?" Nancy asked.

Barbara paled and shook her head. "Of course not! Of course not. What I did was, on Thursday, I counted all of the forks, knives, and spoons that were left and wrote down the amounts. There were 5, 9, and 6. Then I went up and pretended to go to bed, but I stayed up all night listening."

Nancy nodded, the others breathing some sighs of relief.

"I didn't hear anything. I don't know what I would have done if I did, other than wake up Richard. And I would have heard! I left the door slightly open after he fell asleep, and I know from when Leanne was younger that sounds from the kitchen travel upstairs."

"Well, that morning, I went downstairs after the sun was up and counted the silverware again. And there was *less*. There were only 4 forks, 5 knives, and 5 spoons!"

Silence.

"How were there less?" Eleanor asked, clearly rhetorically.

"And you're sure you didn't fall asleep?" Lois asked gently, and Barbara shook her head vigorously.

"No! I didn't! I don't know how it happened. I was going to tell Richard, but he would have said I was crazy."

Lois's eyebrows furrowed; the whole situation was worrying.

"Did you find them later?" Patricia asked, and Barbara nodded. Everyone went silent, waiting expectantly.

"On Saturday, I was combing through the house again when I checked the basement for what must have been the eighth time. By then there was no silverware left, and I didn't want to ask Richard to buy more, so I was desperate. I looked everywhere again, and finally decided to open a lockbox I have down there with my mother's silverware—hers is real silver, so I didn't have it out."

27

The others nodded in understanding; several of them also had inherited or been gifted real silver utensils that they didn't use.

"Well, I opened the box, and to my shock, there they were. On top of the chest of real silver, all of the silverware was there, stacked neatly by type. I'm the only one who knows how to get into the box."

Everyone stared openly in shock.

"It wasn't broken?"

"No! If anyone put them in there, they managed to get the code and relock it afterwards, without anyone knowing they were in the house. I was there the whole time—it wasn't either of my children or Richard. I don't know how it happened."

Barbara was clearly still a bit shaken at this, so Cynthia, who was sitting next to her, took her hands.

"Anybody want to go next?" Cynthia asked, to allow Barbara some time to collect herself.

Patricia and Nancy told somewhat similar stories to Barbara's, though Patricia's dealt with disappearing socks that she found in a big ball in the back of her own closet and Nancy's issue had been with coats that kept moving around the house—seemingly at will, as nobody had been touching them. Both of them mentioned their husbands being skeptical of their claims, assuring them that they had simply misplaced or forgot moving the objects in question.

"I still don't understand it," Nancy had said at the end of her story, "I made it a rule that no one touch any jackets they weren't intending on using to see if they'd stop moving, and they didn't. We all left the house to go out to dinner on Friday and when we came back they'd *still* moved. James thought I was crazy. I had half the mind to call the station, but I'd locked all the doors and windows and none of them were open. Nothing else had been moved. And I thought, who would break into a house just to move around some jackets? So I was under the impression I was going insane."

"Lois, you haven't had anything like this?" Eleanor asked, and Lois shook her head.

"I haven't either."

Eleanor turned to Cynthia.

"I have. That's why Winston told me in the first place," Cynthia revealed, and again any stray voices were silenced.

"It was something like what's been happening to Nancy. Shoes keep on moving around, seemingly of their own accord. You all know I have everyone take their shoes off before they come into the house, so when I started finding shoes anywhere other than the foyer, I was confused. The kids know not to do that, and they're old enough that when I asked I knew they hadn't. Winston asked them too, because he likes everything to be in order. But there wasn't any dirt, or anything else, following them. They were just moved, like someone had picked them up and put them somewhere else."

"After a few days of it, Winston locked all the shoes in a lockbox he'd covered in bells except for the pairs that the kids wore to go to school. He was the only one with the key and he went to the station with it. I went upstairs to the sewing room to repair some clothing that Jules and May had torn, purposefully not listening to any music so I could hear if anyone used the box. There was no sound, but when Winston came home for lunch I heard him shout and ran downstairs. The box was still locked, but there were shoes everywhere— he interrogated me, but he knows when I'm telling the truth, and realised I hadn't done it. I told him I hadn't heard anything and hadn't had any music playing, so now the police are taking the calls more seriously."

Lois had bitten her lip halfway through the story and only just realised that she'd nearly cut herself with her tooth. Consciously letting her jaw loosen, she resisted the urge to leave and go check up on her own home.

"But...half, if not all, of these situations don't seem to involve *people*," she pointed out, and everyone looked at her.

"None of you heard anything and none of you saw anyone, but everything was still moving. How—what could be causing it?"

Nancy opened her mouth to scoff at what Lois was implying on instinct, but said nothing, as she had no other explanation.

"Well, it has to be people," Eleanor said, but she was clearly unsure as she added, "…right?"

In the ensuing silence, Lois looked down and noticed that in her nervousness she'd knitted an entire blanket. She checked it quickly for any poor stitch work, but it didn't have any errors. Blinking, she finished it off and started on a new one, using the new blanket to combat the chill she'd gotten once they'd started on this conversation.

"Well, what with everything the world has seen, I guess it's not too much of a shock that there's something supernatural at play," Nancy finally said.

"Oh, come on." Eleanor scoffed, but her heart wasn't in her words.

"Well, that would explain why nobody saw anything, or heard anything," Patricia said.

"And I didn't. How else would they have gotten in the box?" Barbara asked, and nobody had an answer.

"James has been investigating it to write an article, with a bit more fervor now that something happened to us personally. Apparently, it's happening to a lot of people, and nobody else has seen anyone doing it," Nancy reported.

"So, so it's something here, in Rose Park, that nobody can see or hear, just going into our houses and…and just messing with us?" Lois asked, her voice shaking slightly.

Patricia, who was sitting next to her, patted Lois's knee.

"It would appear so," Cynthia confirmed, her voice sympathetic.

Lois stood up abruptly, putting her knitting work down. "I've got to call my husband."

"Wait!"

"Don't tell him—"

"I'm not going to tell him," she assured all of them as they all objected, "I just need to check in on him." Her voice broke, so they nodded.

She walked over to the phone on the other side of the living room and sat down in the empty chair next to it, all of the others staring at her as she quickly dialed her own number with a shaking hand. The first time she messed up, accidentally not pulling the rotary far enough for one of the numbers, but the second time she got it. Her finger nervously curled around the cord as she held the receiver up to her head, the ringing audible to everyone in the room.

It took a few rings for someone to pick up.

"Hello?"

"Paul?" Lois asked, her voice jumping a bit.

"Lois! You usually don't call during knitting club. Are you alright?"

The others leaned in a bit, trying to hear.

"Yes, I'm fine. I just wanted to see if you were."

"You don't sound fine, Lois. Are you sure nothing is wrong?"

Lois nodded, though he couldn't see her.

"No, nothing's wrong. Are you alright?" Her voice was a bit more forceful this time.

"Everything's great here, Lois. We're listening to music and playing games."

"The kids are alright? Nothing's wrong at all? You're sure?"

There was a pause.

"Yes, everything's fine. I promise. Lois, what is this all about?"

Lois sighed in relief.

"Nothing, nothing. Just making sure."

"*Lois—*"

"I've got to go! I'll see you when knitting is over, alright?"

Another pause, and a sigh.

"Yes, my darling. Have fun. Love you."

"I love you too."

Her poignant tone and brief pause left room for Paul to start, "Lois, please—"

"Thank you! Goodbye." Lois quickly hung up.

"Well?"

"He says everything is fine."

From the way she walked back to her seat it was apparent she wasn't entirely calmed.

"Well, Paul would never lie to you," Nancy assured her soothingly.

"I know, but he's not at the house as much as I am. He might not notice if something was moved."

Nancy couldn't argue with that.

"No, I don't think Brian would notice either. He's distracted enough as it is normally," Eleanor agreed, clearly a bit nervous that this would start happening to her as well.

Only Lois picked her knitting back up as worried conversations took place, each of the other wives asking who was next to her if they had any ideas, if they had left anything out of their stories, if anything else was happening.

"I don't think we should call the station if we notice anything more," Cynthia said above the din after having considered it for a little while, and everyone turned to her.

"If it's truly something supernatural, the police can't do anything about it. What we'll have to do is keep track of it for ourselves."

Several people gasped, so Cynthia quickly clarified, "Nothing too big! Firstly, we should move to four meetings a week. Will Wednesday work for you, Patricia?"

She nodded, so Cynthia continued, "I can have Winston tell me about people who call cases in, so I'll keep track of where they are and what area of the neighborhood they're focused on. All I ask is that you all keep a diary of any strange things that happened. I know some of you have very *curious* husbands, so I want you all to keep it in the format of a dream journal. Start out every entry with 'last night I dreamt,' and then write down all the details. When you have time, you can also go to the library and see if you can find any information about this kind of phenomena. But, don't check out any books."

The wives all nodded, and at this point Cynthia looked pointedly at Eleanor and Lois.

"Nothing has happened to either of you, but if anything *does* start happening, call me, alright? And then start doing the dream diary. I recommend you don't tell your husbands about it." Before either of them could say anything, Cynthia looked specifically at Lois, who was already pale.

"Lois, I know that Paul will know that something is wrong. If he asks, I know Winston's probably told him about this when they've spent time together or when he's stopped by your store—just tell him you're worried about how people's homes seem to be being robbed. If you tell him the truth, he won't believe you."

Lois lost all colour in her face at this but nodded. Being independent was by no means a foreign concept to her, but in a situation like this, she would have greatly preferred to be able to tell the person she loved most in the world. Instead of saying anything, Lois nodded, and her focus went back to her knitting as conversation picked up again.

The time went by fast, but Lois had managed to finish a third blanket by the time everything had wrapped up. Everyone said their goodbyes and filtered out at about 10:00, Cynthia holding Lois back until the others had all gone.

"Lois."

Cynthia managed to get the distracted woman to make real eye contact for the first time in at least two hours.

"Hmm?"

Cynthia looked at her searchingly for a few moments.

"I know you like to be in control of things, but it'll be alright. We're all in this together, okay?"

Lois bit her lip, but nodded.

"*Lois.*"

"Yes, I know."

Cynthia gave a small smile and wrapped Lois in a hug. Lois hadn't expected it, stiffening a bit before leaning into it and wrapping her arms around Cynthia as well. The embrace was only interrupted when the door opened and the two women jumped and broke apart, turning to see Winston staring as he closed the front door.

"Lois! I didn't expect you to be here so late. You're always so tightly on schedule. Paul might be worried about you." He greeted with a smile, giving Lois a quick hug.

Being her husband's best friend, Winston had gotten quite familiar with her. Cynthia put on a smile, and Lois quickly did the same.

"Yes, I was just talking with Cynthia about something. I've just finished some more blankets for the store tonight."

"Oh, yes, I've seen them in the front rack. Paul says you knock at least one out every club night."

Lois nodded as she pulled on her jacket, anxious to get back.

"Your shoes are where you left them?" Winston suddenly asked, much more serious than his previous tone.

"Oh, yes, they're right here," she assured him, pretending that she hadn't noticed the tone, and pulled them on.

"Good. Alright. Have a good night, Lois. Tell Paul I say the same."

Lois smiled.

"I will. I left some cookies here if you'd like."

Winston grinned.

"Excellent! Thank you very much."

"Goodnight." Lois said, and they both mirrored the sentiment as she left.

Chapter 4

Lois closed and locked the door immediately upon getting home, quickly taking off her shoes and hanging her coat on the rack. The house was quiet, but it was past her children's' bedtime so she wasn't too worried by this. She put the tin with the remaining cookies on the table in the kitchen before quickly going window to window to make sure they were all locked. She finished the kitchen, the playroom, the dining room, the laundry room, and headed into the living room last. Lois made a beeline for the windows without paying attention to anything else in the room.

"It's almost 10:20, why are you late?"

Lois gasped and jumped about a foot in the air before turning to see Paul quickly walking over to her from the sofa chair he'd been sitting in, concern clear on his face.

"I didn't mean to scare you, darling, are you alright?"

Lois nodded, a hand over her chest as she tried to slow her heartbeat. Paul quickly pulled her into a hug. After a few moments, her hand left her heart and she wrapped her arms around him, burying her face in his chest and gripping him tightly.

"Lois? Lois, what's wrong?" Paul murmured at her grip, but she didn't reply.

He waited until her grip eased to pull back, which took at least two full minutes. She had steadied her expression, but her eyes revealed that she was still scared of…something.

"Lois, you sounded terrified on that phone call. Please— what's wrong?"

At his soft pleading she had half a mind to tell him everything, but Cynthia's voice came into her head: *He won't believe you.* She swallowed hard, and Paul could tell already that she wasn't going to give him the full story. His eyebrows furrowed; Lois never kept secrets from him.

"Cynthia told me about the calls the station has been getting, about people's things being moved or going missing."

Paul didn't have to wonder what more there could be to that. He had Lois sit down on the couch and positioned himself right next to her, leg to leg. One of his hands was in hers, the other on her arm.

"Lois, have you noticed anything moving or going missing? You know you can tell me anything, right?"

Lois bit her lip as she stared into his eyes, the green of them warm and inviting. She wanted to tell him. She wanted to tell him—

"I haven't, but I worry I will." She said instead, truthfully.

"Is that why you were going to the window?"

"I was making sure all of them are locked. I already know the ones in the girls' rooms are locked, but some of the ones down here weren't. And I made sure the doors were all locked."

His hand travelled from her arm to her face, gently cupping her cheek. The hand he held was shaking.

"I'll bring some new locks home tomorrow and we can add them on. And I'll buy some long screws from Harold to replace any shorter ones our current locks are using."

Lois nodded with a small smile, and Paul brought her into his arms again.

They walked upstairs together after locking the living room windows and checked all the windows upstairs before getting ready for bed. Lois was clearly still nervous, so Paul went into the attic and dug out a bat he sometimes used to play ball with the girls to put beside their bed. Lois pretended to be reassured by this, but she knew that whatever was causing this was not going to be stopped by a baseball bat. They finally crawled into bed at half past eleven, tangled in each other's arms.

Lois woke up at 4:30 AM, half an hour before her regular time. After gently extracting herself from Paul's arms and legs, Lois used this extra time to give the entire house a once over. Nothing was out of the ordinary; even the cutlery was all in the right order. Once she was sure that nothing had happened yet, Lois got ready for the children, having everything set by the time they came downstairs.

"Mommy, where are the apple rings?" Mary asked after her mother had put a plate in front of her.

"Hmm?"

"On Tuesdays, you always make us oatmeal, pineapple, toast, and apple rings. Where are the apple rings?"

Lois blinked before putting on a smile.

"I'm sorry, honey, I was worried they'd be cold and then I lost track of time. I'll make them now." Mary smiled in response, but Linda looked at her mother with silent concern.

Mary had already finished breakfast by the time Lois had made the apple rings but stayed to finish those off as well. That put her a bit behind schedule, as it took her more time to make her bed on her own as compared to Linda. Lois had to go help her, which meant that the dishes were left unwashed by the time Harold had arrived and picked the girls up for school. She quickly grabbed the newspaper and headed up to wake her husband, deciding to just do all the dishes at once.

Paul woke immediately at her voice, blinking as he turned to her.

"Lois? Is it time to get up?"

She nodded, the newspaper still in her hand. He furrowed his brows.

"Is that the paper?"

She looked down at her hand, clearly having not been aware of it being there.

"Oh. Yes."

He gave her a questioning look, but she simply stood up and headed for the door. He stared as she walked out, only being pulled out of his thoughts when his alarm went off at 7:30.

Lois had his plate set out just as he was walking down the stairs, the newspaper now next to it like it usually was. She put her own plate down as he greeted her, eyebrows furrowing when he saw that the sink still had the kid's dishes in them.

"Darling, how are you feeling?"

Her eyes met his with a wide look. From the way she

37

reacted he'd think he'd asked if she'd dented the car.

"I'm fine."

He nodded slowly, pulling his mug to him and going to take a drink of—nothing.

"Did you make the coffee, love?"

She sprang up.

"Oh! Yes." She took the mug somewhat abruptly from his hand and went over to the coffee maker, pouring it in. She handed it to him and he took a sip.

At his expression, she quickly asked, "What?"

"It's cold. When did you brew this?"

Lois blinked, sighing slightly in relief for a reason Paul couldn't imagine.

"Oh. I must have brewed it while I made the kids breakfast. I'm sorry, darling, I can put some in a pot and heat it up on the stove if you want—"

"Lois." Paul stood and put his hands on her shoulders. She flinched slightly, and he blinked with concern.

"Lois, we've lived here for years, and I can't remember the last time you were this distracted. Can you please tell me what's going on?"

To Paul's surprise, Lois started to cry. He immediately pulled her into his arms and walked her out of the kitchen and into the living room, sitting down on the couch and pulling her onto his lap. She hugged him tightly, her body shaking as she sobbed into his shoulder.

Paul, at a bit of a loss of how to help a problem he didn't even know, defaulted to humming as he gently rocked her back and forth. It took several minutes for her to grow quiet, sniffing as Paul hummed along to *Goodnight Sweetheart*—their song, played for their first dance at their wedding.

Once he'd finished the song, he kissed the top of her head before pulling back enough to see her face. Her tears were easily tracked down her face due to the mascara and eyeliner that had come down with them, smudging on Paul's—thankfully dark—button up. Her lip was quivering slightly as he put his forehead to hers.

"Lois, you can tell me anything," he promised, his voice a

soft murmur. She took a deep breath.

"I can't stop thinking about what Cynthia said."

Paul took this to mean about the break-ins—Lois, in a way, had also meant this, but the phrase still running in her mind was 'he won't believe you.'

"I'm going to replace all the short screws and install the extra locks today, I promise."

She nodded. He leaned forward to kiss her and was pleasantly surprised when she leaned into it, her hand trailing up to his cheek. She only broke away when her internal clock went off, alerting her that it was 8:10.

"You have to get to work!" She exclaimed as she pulled away, Paul's eyes still closed.

"What?"

"You're going to be late!"

She leapt up from his lap and ran to get his keys and lunch while he got up and got his shoes and coat on. Lois corralled him into the garage, but she wasn't pushing him to get in the car as much as she usually did. In fact, as she put the lunch in the car and handed him his keys with a shaky hand and a reluctant expression, he got the distinct impression she didn't want him to leave.

"Do you want me to just get the locks and come right back?"

"No, of course not."

Her expression told him the opposite.

"You need to take care of the store. It'll be alright until you bring them home after work."

He got into the driver's seat but leaned out the window, gaze matching hers.

"Are you sure?"

No. "Yes."

He nodded slowly, biting his lip.

"Alright. And, before I forget, you got some makeup on your face."

Lois gave a nervous chuckle, having already realised this.

"Oh! Thank you, I'll wash it off right after this."

He nodded and went to start the car.

39

"Love, these are your keys." He held up the keyring, showing that the nearly identical set had a mint green 'L' instead of a deep blue 'P.'

"Oh! I'll go get yours!" She exclaimed, taking them from his hands and running off. He ran his hands through his hair and massaged the bridge of his nose, having half a mind to just refuse to go to the store and stay here to make sure she felt safe. He was trying to think of what to say when she came back in with the proper keys and pressed them into his hand.

"There you go. Be safe."

"Okay. I'll see you a little after five," he said wistfully before he turned on the car and got it in gear.

"I love you!" She called quickly, and he turned to say it back only to be silenced by her leaning through the window and kissing him.

"I love you too," he murmured when she pulled back, giving her a smile. She smiled back, but as he drove off, all he could think about were her eyes. She was still scared of something, and he got the feeling that it wasn't just the possibility of someone breaking into the house.

Chapter 5

Paul opened up the McCarthy General Store at 8:37, seven minutes later than the listed time. He'd seen that someone was already waiting when he parked, and upon walking up he'd realised it was Brian.

"Good morning, Brian. I hope you haven't been waiting long." Paul let the man go in first before heading behind the counter.

"Only a few minutes. I just need to get some sugar."

"Oh, is Eleanor making something?" Paul asked as he watched Brian finally locate and approach the wall where Paul kept the sacks of sugar.

"No, I don't think so—she just said she was out."

Paul furrowed his eyebrows.

"She was just in here yesterday. She picked up sugar with a few other spices."

Brian nodded as he carried the sack up to the counter.

"I know, she told me, but we're out of it. Said she poured the bag out into our jar and everything, and I used some when I made tea last night, but this morning it was all gone. Eleanor went all pale when I said I didn't know what happened to it but she went off to call someone before I could ask why," he explained as Paul rang him up.

"That's interesting. What do you think happened to it?"

"Oh, I don't know," he replied as he paid, "Eleanor always keeps track of all that. I'm sure there's some reasonable explanation. Maybe the kids ate it."

Brian was too focused on putting his wallet back to notice Paul had written out a receipt and was holding it out to him. He finally took the receipt as he reached for the sugar, nodding and thanking Paul before hurrying out.

Now that Paul was alone he got up to restock any empty shelves, thinking lightly about what Brian had told him. He'd set everything up and started reading the newspaper by the time someone else came in, getting caught midway through an editorial about the rise in people complaining about things moving or going missing in their homes.

"Paul."

Harold's voice reached him before Paul had even looked up. He put the paper down.

"Hello, Harry. I actually have to get some things from you today, we—"

"Did Lois tell you about what they were discussing last night?" He interrupted, strolling right up to the counter with no obvious intention of buying anything.

"Some of it. She said that there's been a lot of things going missing, things Winston told me a bit about."

Harold nodded.

"I just replaced all the screws of the locks in the house yesterday. Patricia said that the socks had been going missing—she was right, but she found them all in a big ball in the closet. I know she wouldn't do that, and I asked the kids, but they didn't know anything about it."

Harold shook his head as Paul blinked.

"What I want to buy are some longer screws, actually. For the same purpose. Lois' pretty scared about the whole thing." Harold and he were friends, but Paul stopped himself before mentioning that he thought there was something she wasn't telling him—that seemed too private to share, at least with him. Harold nodded in understanding, clearly oblivious to Paul's omission.

"The locks we have are good. I don't know how anyone would be getting in. I left some powder by the sills so we could see if anyone used them. Might want to have Lois do that, too."

Paul nodded.

"Thanks for the idea, Harry, I think I will. Did you come in for anything else?" he asked, half expecting Harold to still want to buy locks.

"Just checking. I think something more is going on here. Patricia keeps telling me she thinks someone must have been breaking in when I ask, but I don't think she believes that either. Lots of people who come to the shop are saying their wives are missing things and moving things. They're just complaining, but if their wives are anything like Patricia, they'd know if something had moved."

"Lois would," Paul agreed, and Harold nodded.

"Anyway. Just wanted to know what you knew. Thanks. Bring your car around later and I'll show you how to put in the part. It came in. I told Lois to tell you, but you didn't call."

"Oh, alright, I'll bring it around lunch."

Harold nodded before turning and leaving.

Alone with his thoughts, Paul began to really think about what Harold had said. If he was right and his kids hadn't done it, it would appear that someone had broken into his house just to move around some socks. It must have been the kids, too scared to tell when they saw how upset their parents had gotten. Right?

A nagging feeling still kept at Paul as thought about it; Harold always seemed to know when anyone was lying to him. He was perceptive about that, but Paul also knew Harold was quick to assume something larger was at play. Before Paul could dismiss that, however, he thought back to Brian's story: a whole bag of sugar gone in just a night. Even someone like Brian should have been able to notice the effect eating a bag of sugar would have on two kids, but where else could it have gone?

Paul went back to reread the editorial. It was vague—perhaps one line about a specific story while most were generalised—but they were definitely similar. People either had things moved or things disappear, but none of them caught anyone doing it. It would seem they did have a delinquent in Rose Park, which he supposed was inevitable, but whoever it was certainly knew what they were doing.

In the hours up until noon a few women stopped by to pick up various things but offered no conversation. They all seemed to be concerned—in a hurry to get back to their homes. It wasn't until he was getting ready to temporarily close the shop so he could bring the car to Harold when a voice rang out that actually wanted to speak to him.

"Paul! Where are you going?" Winston asked as he walked in, seeing Paul pulling on his jacket.

"Winston? Shouldn't you be at the station?"

Paul grabbed his keys.

"I've got my radio on me. What about you? You never leave the store during work hours."

Paul shook his head.

"I have to bring my car to Harry to get a part replaced, and I need to pick up longer screws to replace the ones in the current locks. Lois is really worried about all this break-in business."

"She should be. I'll come with you," Winston warned as they left the store, locking the door before heading to Paul's car. Winston's cruiser was parked in front of the shop, but he hopped in with Paul.

"If I leave the car, people might get less upset about you being closed," Winston explained when the other turned to him, and Paul nodded.

"Sure. Winston, what can you tell me about this? Harold told me about a problem Patricia had with socks, and apparently a whole bag of sugar went missing right out of Eleanor's sugar pot."

Winston was silent for a few moments as Paul started up the car and drove off.

"Well," He said, taking a deep breath, "I can tell you a few things. Other than all those calls we've been getting, something actually happened at my house. I haven't told anyone, but Cyn probably told all the girls, including Lois. Shoes in the house kept getting moved. At first I thought it was Jules or May, but I asked them and let's just say it wasn't them. Cynthia was just as upset about it, so one morning after the kids left I locked all the rest of the shoes in a lockbox I'd taped bells to and kept the key. Cyn stayed home, so I knew she'd hear it if anyone who didn't know what they were doing touched it, and I was the only one with a key."

"When I came back home for lunch to check on it, shoes

44

were *everywhere*. I must have shouted because Cynthia came running downstairs, but she said she hadn't heard anything and hadn't had any music on. When I checked, the box was still locked."

Paul was silent through all of this, not replying when Winston finished. His friend had his head in his hands as Paul drove up to edge of town where Harold's shop was, glancing over before Harold came out and cleared him to drive in to the garage.

"Who do you think it is?" Paul asked as he turned the car off, and Winston shook his head before looking back up.

"I don't know. Someone who knows what they're doing."

They climbed out of the car as Harold patted the hood.

"Hello Paul, Winston."

Winston patted him on the shoulder as he walked over to the side and leaned against the wall.

"Here's the part." Harold showed Paul, opening up the hood as the owner followed him.

"After this replacement, just keep an eye on it when you change the oil or do any other tune up. If it gets too dirty it'll bust again."

Paul nodded, leaning against the edge of the car as Harold got his tools.

"Did you tell him about it?" Paul asked, purposefully vaguely in case Harold did not want to tell Winston about Patricia's problem.

"Yep."

"The socks? Yeah." Winston backed up, and Paul nodded.

"Of the group, only you haven't had a problem yet, if Eleanor's sugar went missing," Winston added.

"You're a shrinking minority," Harold commented as he worked, "More people came in before you did complaining about similar things. Only one didn't seem to have any problems. At least not any he shared."

"Do you think it's one person?" Paul asked.

"There's so many that it can't be. But nobody's seen a damn thing, and I know most of these housewives are eagle-eyed. Someone should have seen something, but nobody's come forward and I can't see why they'd hide it."

Paul shrugged, "Maybe if it was their kid?"

"No kid did this," Harold and Winston said in unison, glancing at the other in mild surprise.

"You already know what I think," Harold said, occupying himself with his work. A few moments of silence.

"What?" Paul asked.

"Harry thinks it's something not human," Winston scoffed. He was always incredibly dismissive of anything even remotely unscientific, which mixed poorly with Harold's more spiritual opinions. Paul knew he didn't believe a word of it.

"What would it be, then?"

"At the very least, it's a gang of professionals," Winston reasoned.

"Do you really think there are professional criminals here?" Paul asked, and when Winston shrugged he turned to Harold.

"I don't know everything that's out there. But I know nobody in the house did it, and I know everything was locked."

Harold's words permeated the air as they were left in silence. Paul did not want to consider something unknowable to even exist, so he shut out the idea. For now, he was operating on the assumption that it was a group of highly skilled pranksters. It sounded ridiculous, but it was more realistic than some unknown force. Right?

"All fixed up," Harold announced, closing the hood just as Paul stepped up and out of the way, "Just keep it clean."

Paul nodded, clearly distracted.

"You'd better get back to the shop," Winston said, voice low and thoughtful.

"Yes—wait. Harold, I need long screws. Longest you have in the typical width. I need them for my locks." Harold nodded, walking off and leaving Paul and Winston alone.

"Winston—"

"I don't know," he replied, already knowing what Paul was going to ask. That was not the answer Paul was hoping for.

His hand tapped against his legs as Winston ran his hand through his hair, messing up the coif.

"I don't know, I don't know…there's been no evidence anywhere. No signs of break-ins. I've had the boys check out calls now, and nobody's found anything. How did they get in the damn lock box without making any noise? Without a key?"

Paul had no answer.

"I don't think it's something supernatural, but until I find any evidence—any evidence *at all*—even Harold's kooky ideas might be worth a listen. He's not *right*, but maybe there's a shred of truth in there. Something that'll lead me to the actual, human answer."

Paul ran a hand through his own hair as Harold walked back in carrying a paper bag.

"Here. Six inches, reinforced. Nobody'll be able to kick through any of those locks and it'll take a hell of a time to unscrew them."

Paul nodded and took the bag, reaching into his pocket for his wallet. Harold put his hand on Paul's shoulder and he stopped.

"Just take them."

"What?"

"Just take them. I know Lois is scared. You already paid for the part, you can have the screws. They're pretty cheap anyway."

Paul blinked.

"I—thank you, Harry."

Harold nodded, patted his shoulder, and gave a nod to Winston before disappearing into his shop.

Neither man spoke on the drive back to the general store, Paul finally pulling back in and reopening the shop at 12:46. Paul had just gotten the door open when the phone started ringing, so he made a beeline for the desk as Winston wandered through the store.

"Hello?"

"Paul?"

Paul quickly sat down. "Yes, dearest?"

"Someone told me you weren't at the shop. Did you go out?"

A sigh of relief.

"Oh, yes, I just brought the car to the garage to get the part replaced."

"Oh! Oh good. I forgot to tell you about it, Harry told me that it was ready."

Paul was reminded of what Harry had said earlier, about how he'd told Lois; Paul bit his lip. It was not like Lois to forget anything.

"It's alright, honey. He dropped by this morning, no time lost. I got the screws as well, so when I come home after closing I'll bring the locks and we can install them and replace the old screws. Is that all?"

A pause.

"Yes, I just wanted to be sure you were alright. I love you."

"I love you, too. Bye, darling."

His hand hesitated slightly before replacing the receiver on the phone's base.

"How's Lois?" Winston asked, drawing Paul out of his thoughts.

"She said she's fine. Someone phoned her to say I was out, and she wanted to know why."

Winston walked over to the counter and leaned against it.

"Is she worried?"

Paul nodded.

"She didn't say anything, but she seemed like something was bothering her. This whole thing—do you think the girls told her about all that with things being moved and lost without any trace of who did it?"

Winston gave him a look and Paul took a deep breath.

"Yeah, yeah. Of course they did." Paul ran a shaking hand through his hair before holding his head in his hands.

"Paul, I know you don't want to believe it, and I don't want to, but there might be something organised behind this. Some kind of masterminds."

Paul looked up enough that his eyes became visible above

his hands.

"Every time I think something's off I've been running off to the station. Most mornings I get there at 2 or 3 AM now, needing to get back so I can at least try to solve this. I can't think of a single easy explanation for how anyone got in the lockbox beyond some criminal mastermind somehow breaking in and muffling every single bell just to scatter my shoes and relock the box. Which is insanity. I don't think it's something supernatural, but I can't think of a reasonable explanation. I'm going to keep trying to find one but keep an eye out. Lois'll definitely notice if something is missing or moved."

Paul nodded, sighing.

"She sounded scared."

Winston patted him on the shoulder.

"I'd better be getting back to the station. I'll see you later."

"Alright. Bye, Winston." Paul said through his hands, watching as he left the store.

Chapter 6

Linda and Mary came home to find the door locked. They knocked and Lois quickly hurried over and opened it, letting them in before relocking it.

"How was school?" Lois asked with a smile.

"Good!" Mary replied, and Linda nodded in agreement. Mary proceeded to tell her mother all about her day while Linda watched the woman closely. Lois wasn't paying as much attention as she usually did—she paid enough that Mary didn't notice and enough to reply, but something was clearly distracting her. When Mary leapt up and ran off to play music, Linda finally spoke.

"Mom?"

"Yes, honey?" Lois asked, beginning to wash Mary's plate.

"Are you alright?"

Lois immediately stiffened. She really had to start making it less obvious how upset she was.

"Yes, dear, why?"

"You seem distracted."

Lois quickly finished the dish and put it in the rack to dry before turning and sitting down next to Linda.

"A few people I know have been losing things, and I'm just concerned for them. That's all."

"Is that about all the people who think someone's breaking in?"

Lois internally winced, having hoped the kids wouldn't have to worry about it.

"Well, yes. But nobody's seen anyone, and when people have lost something they seem to find it a few days later. So, I don't think we're in any danger. Just in case, your father and I are going to be adding some locks."

Linda nodded, satisfied enough with her mother being

worried about possible break-ins.

"Alright. I'm going to do my homework."

Lois smiled.

"Okay, honey. Tell me if you want any help with it."

Linda nodded and excused herself, letting her mother occupy herself with cleaning the dishes while she went up to her room to do her work.

Paul couldn't wait until five to close the shop, lasting only until 4:45. He locked up and drove straight home, surprising Lois when he pulled in at 5:00. She opened the door to the garage as he was getting out of the car, clearly surprised.

"It's not 5:15, is it?" She asked, clearly not sure, and he shook his head.

Worries about her not being aware of the time were filed away as he explained, "I wanted to get the locks in as soon as possible. Winston stopped by and made me more worried about the situation."

To his surprise, Lois walked over and wrapped her arms around him. He hesitated for a second before hugging her back—every other time he'd come home early, she'd been concerned and clearly against the idea of it.

"Okay. Let's do it." Lois cleared her throat as she pulled back. Paul pulled the bag of screws and locks out of the car, handing them to his wife before getting his toolbox off a nearby shelf.

Mary had heard the drill once they started on the first lock but ignored it until they came in to the living room to work on the windows. She stopped the gramophone and watched for a few seconds before getting up and walking over.

"What are you doing?"

"We're just adding some locks, honey," Paul explained. Lois nodded when Mary turned to check with her.

"Why?"

"The house is safer this way."

"Why?"

"It's harder for other people to get in."

"Why?"

"They can't open the doors and windows."

51

"Oh. Okay."

Mary moved away slightly but watched as they added a lock that mounted to the sill to each window in the living room, needing to use the shorter screws from earlier locks on the window frame itself due to its thickness.

They were followed by Mary throughout the first floor, down into the basement, and up to the second floor—where Linda joined for a little while in interest—before finishing up by climbing into the attic. After every window and door in the house had additional locks added, the children went back to their earlier activities.

The two adults retreated to the kitchen upon putting away the tools. Lois quickly finished dinner—this meal not missing anything from the typical Tuesday—while Paul set the table and helped with anything she hadn't already had done by the time he arrived.

Dinner was unusually quiet, Mary making the biggest contribution to the conversation. However, it didn't take long for even her to notice how distracted both of her parents were and settle with talking to Linda instead. Linda had hoped that her mother would be more relieved once they'd put the locks in; Lois being nervous made her nervous.

She became more nervous upon dinner ending and Paul murmuring something to Lois, at which point they went throughout the house and put pink baby powder on every windowsill, telling their children not to touch it and that it "was for ants."

Linda went to bed a little early that night, pushed on at the insistence of her parents—they explained they were going retire early as well; by Mary's regular bedtime of 8:00 everyone was in bed. Paul sat up and waited for Lois to get her makeup off, staring at her through the open bathroom door. Her foot tapped silently on the small carpet in front of the sink, her hands shaking as she scrubbed at her face. She was distracted. He was about to ask if she was hurting herself when she toweled herself off and came to bed.

Lois and Paul moved in unison to wrap around each other. They ended up with Lois on his chest, legs tangled and arms wrapped around each other. Paul reached over and turned out the light before they got too comfortable, closing his eyes as Lois nuzzled into him. The locks being on everything did not sooth him as much as he hoped it would, but at the very least Lois had stopped shaking. He gave her a squeeze and kissed the top of her head before letting himself drift off, unable to know how long Lois was staring into the darkness before sleep finally took her.

It was fully dark when Lois shot up in bed. Something was wrong—or, maybe it was just a nightmare. Paul shifted in his sleep, his arms wrapping around her waist and his head resting on her lap. She glanced over at the clock to see it was 4:31 in the morning and groaned softly. Her heart was racing and she was fully awake, so she decided to just get up.

After the delicate process of extricating herself from her husband without waking him, Lois went through her morning routine and walked downstairs fully dressed at 5:10. She prepared breakfast to be cooked but had downtime before it actually had to be put on the burners, which she spent obsessively checking every object in the house for misplacement.

Everything was in order.

Mary and Linda woke up to their regular Wednesday breakfast, their mother acting almost entirely normal. She was a little quieter than normal, but otherwise her nerves appeared to be gone. Linda was calmed by this, assuming the presence of the locks was helping.

After telling them about her knitting club meeting that night and that dinner would thus be at 5:30, she stood with them waiting for Harold's car. He gave her a meaningful look as he arrived, sending a short wave her way as Linda and Mary hurried to get in. Lois gave him a false smile he saw right through, but he wasn't in the position to comment on it.

She took the newspaper, put it on the table, and took a deep breath before heading upstairs. Paul sat up the moment Lois entered the bedroom, surprising her.

"Paul, are you alright?"

"When did you wake up, love?" His voice was hoarse with

sleep, but Lois got the impression he hadn't woken up very recently.

"Half past four."

He groaned, reaching his arms out for her. She walked over and let him pull her into a hug, sighing softly as he nuzzled into her and pressed kisses to the top of her head.

"I'm worried, too," he murmured, "But Winston is going to catch whoever is doing this. It's nothing to be concerned about. Just some pranksters."

Lois stiffened almost imperceptibly, biting her lower lip and shutting her eyes tightly. She'd known that he couldn't possibly think it was something supernatural, but hearing it come out of his mouth was like a slap in the face. Cynthia was right. He wouldn't believe her.

"I know, dear." She forced herself to respond, deciding that it was right for her to act like nothing was wrong. Worrying the kids and her husband would solve nothing. Ultimately, it would only put her in a position where she'd either have to lie to them or tell a truth they wouldn't believe. The choices soured her stomach, but she didn't see any other way.

Lois pulled away from Paul, softly kissing him on the forehead before stepping into the bathroom to fix her lipstick. He hadn't even managed to get into the room to start his shower by the time she was hurrying back downstairs.

Breakfast was quiet.

"I have a knitting club meeting today. At Patricia's," Lois informed Paul after a period of uncomfortable silence, his eyes never leaving her. The paper sat beside his plate untouched.

"Is there usually a meeting on Wednesdays?" He asked, eyebrows furrowing.

"It's not out of the ordinary."

She felt this was less sinful than out and out lying and saying 'yes.'

"Ah. Well. Hopefully you'll have a good time." His eyebrows furrowed slightly, and she avoided his gaze in favour of focusing on her plate. He'd wanted to spend time with her after work, but now she'd be off with the other housewives. They'd likely rile themselves up and she'd come home even more worried. Paul frowned.

"How was your last meeting? Aside from the gossip," he asked, hoping to sedate her. Paul was hoping they hadn't spent the whole meeting talking about the alleged break-ins.

"Oh! I finished three blankets."

Lois rose very suddenly from the table and disappeared to get her knitting bag. He blinked, staring at where she'd been before looking at the doorway she'd disappeared through. He'd entirely forgotten about the blankets, but the fact that it had also escaped Lois's mind made worry creep into his consciousness again.

The locks, suffice to say, were not easing her fears.

"Here we are," she said, her voice dripping with a saccharine cheer. Paul almost winced at it as she pulled out a chair and took three blankets from her bag, placing them onto it so he could see.

"One of them was almost done when I'd brought it, I don't think I could knit three whole blankets in one evening. They're ready to take to the store." She turned to him with a small smile, but it fell off when she saw his expression.

"I'll just put them in the car."

Lois was in the garage with the blankets in tow before Paul could protest. He silently cursed to himself, standing up and putting his plates in the sink. She seemed to be taking her time, so he got his shoes and coat on and hurried over to meet her out at the car.

Lois jumped and gasped at the sound of Paul opening the garage door, turning to him with a fearful expression that almost knocked him off his feet.

"You nearly scared the life out of me, surprising me like that!"

Paul blinked.

"All I did was open the door, love."

Usually Lois could hear everything. He'd grown accustomed to her being able to hear his footsteps and tell it was him as he entered a room.

She blinked and shook her head.

"Sorry, I was just trying to figure how many more blankets I should aim for. I think I might be making too many pink ones. Perhaps some more blue ones. Or mint. Mint is such a lovely colour, and you can use it for anyone," she rambled. It was a lie, yes, but a white one.

Paul stepped over and wrapped her up in his arms, deciding to take her word for it. Lois was certainly one to get distracted by something like blanket production, even if it was a bit of a stretch for it to affect her sense of hearing.

"Don't worry about the blankets, my love, everyone adores them. You could make them in any colour you'd like and I'm sure it'd be the same. We sell enough that soon you won't be able to keep up," he assured her in a light tone, and she chuckled. She snaked her arms around him and gave him a squeeze.

"Here are your keys, dearest." Lois broke off the hug as she pressed his keys into his hand. She kissed his cheek as he got into the car, seeing that she'd put the blankets on the passenger's seat.

"I love you," he said, voice trembling slightly with meaning. She blinked, looking at him with mild surprise. She slipped one of her hands into his and gave it a squeeze, a soft smile forming on her face.

"I love you too."

Chapter 7

Once Paul was gone, Lois gave the house another scrupulous check, but nothing was out of order. Her cleaning chores for that day were less laborious than Monday's, so she had the extra time to go over the finances after her daily exercises. Lois's gift for mathematics and nigh obsessive attention to detail lent well to her habit of planning everything for the family. Paul had long relinquished the duty of budgeting to her. He still did the taxes, but Lois did most everything else.

Lois had come up with an unusually specific budget and wrote a copy for Paul before she got up to hang up the laundry, changing into her gardening clothes so she could do something to clear her mind. Budgeting was an enjoyable distraction, but if she got any more to the letter she'd be writing in specific brand names and grocery trip estimates to the cent.

After checking that the front yard's bright blue morning glories and hydrangeas were doing well, she ventured into the backyard. She tended to the food garden first, pruning here and there and watering her plants. Then she checked on the flowers; While Lois had made sure there was plenty of space for the girls to run around, she'd not compromised too much on her need for flowers.

Paul had built her a few trellises, one leaning against the house and the others separating the food garden and flower garden from the main backyard. A few were arches while the others were just acting like walls. Around and on these trellises, Lois was growing irises, delphiniums, hyacinths, harvest bells, columbines, lobelia, sweet pea, and desert bluebells—all of which were blue. The only other flowers Lois had were roses, which grew in abundance all over the trellis structures. They were white roses, but Lois put blue dye in the water she used on them so several of them had taken on a blue hue as well.

Lois hummed as she tended to all her flowers, their presence calming her as she moved a blossom here and pruned a dead tendril there. Overall, none of the plants needed much work—she kept such an obsessively close eye on them that they never got the chance to become an issue.

Lois had just changed when there was a knock at the door, alerting her that her children were back from school. She hurried over and unlocked it for them, grinning upon seeing them.

"How was school today?"

Mary broke into a wide grin.

"We did a test on the multiplication tables and I finished them the fastest, so I won!" Mary tore her backpack off, putting it on a chair and pulling out a Kewpie doll in a little white and blue dress. She giggled, shoving it forwards so that Lois could get a good look.

"Oh, Mary! I'm so proud of you!" Lois bent down and gave Mary a big kiss, wrapping her arms around her and lifting her up into a hug. Unlike Linda, Mary was still young enough that she liked being pulled up into impromptu hugs. Her legs clamped around Lois's waist and she wrapped her arms around her mother's neck. Mary happily nuzzled into Lois, the Kewpie doll held fast in a tight fist. Lois thanked the stars she'd decided to start exercising daily all those years ago.

"How about you, Linda?"

"We're doing editing of our stories. Today we did peer edits and tomorrow we're going to decide what changes we want to make and how we want them to stay the same. Then we're going to hand in both the old copy with the edit marks and then the new story so that the teacher can see what kind of edits we've chosen and grade our changes."

Lois nodded thoughtfully.

"Did you get a lot of edits?"

Linda blushed.

"No."

Lois grinned as Linda quickly added, "Well, I got some.

They're good except for a few strange ones I don't want to do."

"Well, I think part of the exercise is knowing which suggestions *aren't* good, sweetheart. Don't do anything you don't want to do. I trust your writing judgement."

Linda smiled.

"If you'd like, I can go over them with you. Or you can go see your father and run it by him," Lois suggested, carrying Mary into the kitchen and putting her down on a chair. She pouted and murmured an 'aww' at being put down but didn't fuss. Linda sat down beside her as Lois quickly made them a snack of cheese and jam on crackers.

"Daniel wants me to tutor him in math!" Mary blurted out after eating a cracker, suddenly remembering. Lois blinked and smiled.

"Shall I ring the Georgesons?"

Mary nodded furiously. Lois excused herself and went to the phone, calling up the number without even having to think about it.

"Hello?" Came Patricia's voice.

"It's Lois."

"Oh! Hello, Lois! Is this about…tonight?"

Lois got the distinct impression that Patricia was not alone.

"Oh, this is about Daniel, actually. Mary tells me he wants her to show him some math?"

Patricia gave a slight sigh. Lois thought it sounded like one of relief.

"Oh! Alright, just a moment!"

The sound of Patricia shouting "DANIEL?" was audible even with Patricia's head turned away and her hand on the receiver. Lois gave a quiet chuckle in the ensuing pause.

"DA—oh, there you are, honey. Mrs. McCarthy says you want to have Mary show you some ways to improve your math?"

Evidently, he nodded.

"I see! Is it alright if he comes over now? As long as he's back by five."

"Yes, that's good. I'll be waiting for him."

"Alright, I'll send him right over. Goodbye!"

Lois was able to hear Patricia tell Daniel to gather his things before she hung up. Lois replaced the receiver and walked into the kitchen.

"He'll be over soon. Why don't you wait for him on the porch?"

Mary bounced to her feet, following her mother to the door and waiting impatiently for her to unlock it. She squeezed out the moment it was open far enough for her to get through, flouncing down on the porch steps. Somewhat reluctantly, Lois closed the door and decided not to lock it.

Linda decided to go up to her room to do her homework when Mary and Daniel came in, sitting down in the living room. Lois brought them a plate of crackers and cheese before going back into the kitchen, starting on dinner a little early.

Spare ribs took a while, she reasoned, especially with the plum gaze—other excuses floated through her mind. She didn't want to admit her early start was merely a distraction.

The ribs were cooking and she'd nearly finished cooking dumplings with orange marmalade and maraschino cherries when her internal clock informed her it was five o'clock. She wiped her hands off on her apron and walked into the living room, smiling when she saw the packets of math homework finished and Mary at the tail end of an explanation of long division.

"It's five o'clock, dears, time for Daniel to go back home."

Mary pouted but said nothing, knowing it was useless to argue against her mother's clock.

"Do you get it?"

Daniel nodded and gave her a small smile.

"I'll walk you over there, dear," Lois offered, and Daniel nodded.

"Mary, can you ask Linda to watch the stove for me? She knows when to take the dumplings off of the range. And I know how many there are, so don't try anything," Lois added lightly, and Mary gave her an innocent smile.

"Okay. Bye, Daniel!" She took off up the stairs and Daniel

reached for Lois's hand. He was eight, but he was a sensitive boy and Patricia intended on keeping him that way. His older brother Sean was similar, but at a year older he'd managed to get out of his mother's habit of holding his hand.

They started off down the road at a leisurely pace, Daniel as quiet as ever. Lois was fine with the silence, taking the time to gaze at her neighbor's flowerbeds as they went.

"Dad says there's something here." Daniel's voice was soft. Lois got the distinct impression he didn't mean that there was something under their feet or behind the next hedge.

"He says that something else moved the socks. That it's affecting the plants and the energy in the air." Daniel looked up at Lois, who was keeping her expression carefully blank.

"Does he know what it is?"

"No. But he's worried about it."

Lois wasn't sure what to do. She didn't want to worry Daniel, but knowing that Harold believed that this was something supernatural made it difficult not to interrogate the child.

"Your father may be on to something. But I don't know what to tell you," Lois said, truthfully, and Daniel nodded sagely as he looked back forwards. They were nearly at Patricia's house now—she only lived a few houses down, just barely out of view of Lois's.

"My mother doesn't believe him," Daniel added, answering Lois's silent question of why he was telling her all of this. Apparently, Patricia was a better actor than Lois had thought. She'd have to take a page out of her book.

However, as Daniel looked back up at her, big brown eyes showing concern and frustration, Lois couldn't find it in herself to lie to him. At least, not completely.

"I can understand why she doesn't. It's hard to believe. But, at the same time, nobody's seen anything—maybe your dad has a point."

Daniel accepted this answer, nodding. He gave Lois a quick hug when they got to the doorstep just as she knocked on the door. Patricia, hands coated in flour and apron slightly stained, opened it as if she'd been waiting by the window watching them approach.

"Come on in, dear," Patricia said, bending down. Daniel gave her a kiss on the cheek and waved a goodbye to Lois before disappearing into the house.

"I think Mary helped him."

Patricia smiled.

"I'm glad. I'll check over his homework before everyone comes over. Thank you again for letting him come over—you know how Daniel's more artistic than mathematic. Harry's been showing him how to work with his hands, but he likes the guitar."

Lois smiled. It was nice to have a normal conversation. She herself was musically inclined, but much more to singing than playing.

"The only instrument I can play is the piano."

Patricia chuckled.

"Harry's quite the musician."

A timer went off and Patricia straightened, eyebrows rising.

"I've got to take care of that—I'll see you tonight, Lois. Stay safe."

Lois nodded, managing to say goodbye just as Patricia closed the door and hurried off to keep whatever it was that'd just timed off from burning. She turned and walked down the porch, heading somewhat dazedly back to her house.

She should have known Harold would know; Harold seemed to know a lot of things that were beyond the normal. He could always tell when it was going to rain or storm, when someone was upset, if they were lying—and he had an disturbing ability to predict when something terrible was going to happen. He was spiritual, as Paul had once said, though now Lois suspected it was less to do with that and more to do with being tuned in.

She'd have to talk with him about it, however discretely.

Chapter 8

"Mom! You're back! Did something happen?" Mary pulled Lois into the room. She hadn't realised how long she'd been gone—Linda had needed to take the dumplings off and put them on a rack to cool before starting on the sides herself. Paul had arrived at 5:15 and jumping into helping her.

"Oh, I'm sorry, girls, I got caught up talking to Patricia. I'll take it from here. Thank you so much for your help." She took over control of the pans, checking on the ribs and the glaze. Then she turned to Linda, who was making sure her mother had caught up on what she'd missed. Lois smiled.

"You did a wonderful job, honey."

Linda gave her a soft smile before walking out and to her room, Mary following her lead and exiting to the living room. Paul, who'd stayed quiet while the girls were there, waited until everything was under Lois's control before drawing her attention to him with a hand to her shoulder.

"Lois," he murmured. She, hesitantly, turned to look at him.

"Yes?"

"You never seem to be off time, love. What could have possibly distracted you? It's only a few minutes to Patricia's, and the girls said you left at five. Did something happen? Did you see something?"

"Oh, nothing like that, dear. Daniel started talking to me and he's always such a quiet boy, I couldn't not stop to listen to him. And then when Patricia opened the door we started talking, and I suppose I just got distracted, is all. And it's such a lovely afternoon, have you seen the sunset?"

He had in fact seen the sunset, but as lovely as it was, he'd never known something so inconsequential to distract her from her chores. Lois wasn't telling him something, and he hated that she felt like she couldn't talk to him—the thought occurred to him that she was just still scared from the uncertainty of the break—in situation and didn't want to bother him by complaining more than she already had, especially when he couldn't do anything about it. Lois was certainly the type to hold something in if she found it would be easier not to talk about it.

Paul frowned. He still wanted her to tell him, even if it was the same worries every day. If it was bothering her this much, it was the very least he could do to hear her out, even if it was repetitive.

"Are you still worried?"

She looked down at the pans on the range.

Paul blew out a soft sigh, wrapping his arms around her from behind and settling his head on her shoulder. He gently swayed them side to side, just enough to not interrupt her cooking. Pressing gentle kisses to her cheek, he held his tongue. Now wasn't a good time for a heartfelt conversation about her fears and sorrows.

"I'm right here. I'll always be right here."

She leaned back into him and turned to kiss him when a distraction wouldn't compromise the meals, reaching over and turning the heat down as she pulled away. Lois turned to him with a meaningful look in her eyes, biting her lip. He put his hands on her shoulders, nodding slightly and waiting for what he knew had to be an outpouring of her deepest emotions.

"Can you tell the girls it's time for dinner?"

Dinner was almost entirely normal, Mary happily dominating the conversation as she told Paul all about how she'd done her multiplication tables the fastest and how Daniel needed help and how he was good at math, really, he just needed it to be explained to him a different way. Paul found it an easy distraction to listen, Linda adding things here and there about her own day. Lois, who'd already heard everything, was forgiven for her relative silence, and it was left uncommented on.

Linda and Mary excused themselves after they were done eating, Lois immediately rising and beginning to wash the dishes. It was already 6:00 and Lois intended on being quite early to this meeting, wanting to hear about the problems everyone else was having. It was a small comfort that nothing had happened to her yet.

"Lois," Paul said to get her attention, but as she turned to him he knew from her expression he wasn't going to get anything out of her.

"Yes, my love?"

"I just wanted to offer to do the dishes for you. Let you leave earlier." Paul often ended up doing some of the dishes on knitting club nights anyway, as Lois would leave to be there at 6:20 whether they were done or not. He knew she intended on just finishing them when she got home from the meeting, but he always made sure to save her from that inconvenience.

"Are you sure? You've been working at the store all day."

"It's mostly sitting around. You go on. I'll see you when you get back, alright?"

She pretended not to notice the implications in his statement as she kissed him on the cheek, taking off her gloves and hurrying out of the room to get her knitting supplies ready. Paul watched silently as she came back in, put the dumplings in a tin, and took a last sip of water from the glass she'd had at dinner. Then she turned to Paul and wrapped her arms around him, leaning up to kiss him properly—he restrained himself from wrapping his arms around her and getting her dress wet as he returned it, pressing a last kiss to her nose before she turned away and was out of the kitchen.

"Goodbye, dear!" she called, and he didn't have the chance to reply by the time the door was closed. He heard the key in the lock and stared out the window to see her head in the direction of Patricia's, watching until she disappeared.

"You're early, even for you," Patricia noted as a greeting when Lois knocked on the door at 6:07. Lois nodded, heaving a heavy sigh. Patricia took the tin of dumplings from her and led her into the living room, watching as Lois sat down

65

heavily on the end of the couch before walking into the kitchen to heat up the dumplings on a pan.

Lois was occupied by her own thoughts when Patricia came back in, putting the plate of dumplings in the middle of the coffee table.

"Did anything happen?"

"No, god, no. Not yet. I just—it's so hard not to talk to Paul about it." Lois' voice kept quiet and strained. She kept herself from running her hands through her hair, not wanting to mess up the curls.

"I know the feeling, I think. Harold—he, well. I think he knows it's something supernatural. Harold's very with it, you know. He's even been telling the kids this or that about it, and I have to pretend like I don't believe him. I can't do it in front of him, he'd know, but…if I talk with him about it I know that he'll do something rash like worry the boys or send us away to my mother's. I can't let him do that. I need to know what's happening with all of you, I can't just pretend that it's nothing while he stays here and minds the shop as things possibly get worse. I want to talk with him, but I don't even know how much he'd believe."

Lois held her tongue. That must have been Patricia's fear talking—she was pretty sure Harold would believe most anything you said so long as he knew you weren't lying.

"It's hard to know what they will or won't believe with something like this."

There was a knock at the door and Patricia was up, excusing herself before she could ask about what Paul thought about all this. Lois considered this a blessing, though she knew it'd come up later when everyone was talking husbands. With a sigh, she started on a new blanket.

Cynthia came first, then Nancy, then Eleanor and Barbara. Eleanor hadn't brought any sweets to eat, shaking her head when Patricia asked. It wasn't like any of them were very hungry in the first place, but it'd become a bit of a tradition.

"It's my sugar," She explained as they sat down, "It's all gone missing. A whole bag yesterday. Brian picked more up but it's all gone again, and this time some of my spices went with it. He picked up more and finally noticed the problems going on, but he has this idea in his head that it's the kids eating it. It's like he doesn't want to notice anything! Though I wouldn't put it past him to be oblivious to what would happen to Stuart and Peter after two bags of sugar. He barely notices when they're in the house."

"You haven't told him anything, have you?" Cynthia asked.

Eleanor shook her head. "I couldn't tell him a thing even if I wanted to. He's more blind than my mother, and her glasses are as thick as my pinky. There's no point in bothering him with something like this when all he'll do is dismiss it."

There were murmurs of agreement from around the room; James was convinced it wasn't supernatural, Richard wouldn't want to hear a thing about it even if Barbara had wanted to tell him, Winston was even more convinced than James that there had to be a natural explanation for it—and none of them would believe their wives if they told them otherwise.

Lois refrained to comment. She ignored the pit in her stomach this consensus caused, instead consciously taking comfort in the fact that she was not alone in being unable to vent to her partner. Patricia stayed silent as well, seemingly not wanting to bring up the idea that Harold may or may not be on their side of thinking.

Nancy took this chance to clear her throat, gathering everyone's attention as she reached into her purse and pulled out a thick volume. She held it up for them all to see.

"I found something at the library that you'll all find interesting."

"I thought I told you not to check anything out of the library." Cynthia chided.

"Well, you'll be happy to hear I didn't check this out."

"*Nancy*."

"What?" The faux innocence in her voice made Patricia giggle.

"Alright, Nance, what is it?" Cynthia sighed. Nancy grinned.

"This is *Beings of the Beyond*. Most of the books at the library that are about things like this are concerned with ghosts and movie monsters, but this one has something pertinent. I found it on the bottom shelf in the back."

Nancy cleared her throat and turned to a page she'd marked with a handkerchief.

"'Beings that are beyond our mortal plane, beyond are understanding, are known as the Eldritch. The Eldritch do not follow the natural law of our world. They are incomprehensible, unknowable, and impossible. They can make the inconceivable happen at the greatest of ease, with seemingly no rhyme or reason. They are rarely seen, only observed by the effects of their actions.'" Nancy read, snapping the book shut with a flourish.

"That must be it, then!"

"Eldritch. Eldritch. I think I've heard that word somewhere," Patricia murmured, mostly to herself.

"If that's the case, then there's nothing we can do."

"Did we ever really think there was anything we could?"

"Has anything happened to you yet, Lois?" Cynthia asked once the conversation died down, and everyone turned to her.

"No, not yet."

"You're lucky," Nancy said immediately as the others nodded in agreement, "It's nothing but trouble trying to make sure everything's in check without alerting James to it. Now he's on my back whenever something's obviously out of place, interrogating me about if I'd seen anything. He thinks the best place to get evidence for a story about it is our house, since Winston isn't sharing anything."

They all turned to Cynthia, who straightened.

"It was difficult enough to get Winston to tell me about this in the first place. He was all shut lip until it actually happened to us—I've had to weasel all my information out of him. I don't know if there's any more evidence, except that he's so frustrated I assume there must not be."

The wives shook their heads, but there was nothing they could do about that.

"What *do* you know then, Cynthia?"

"I know it's still happening to a lot of people, but not from Winston. Jules and May come home talking about how their friends' mothers are all up in a tizzy about things going here and there, and how they're worried they're going to start losing their things."

"Thank the stars Linda and Mary haven't come home talking about that," Lois said softly, and several other mothers agreed. It appeared that it was only occurring to the older children who had more to worry about: Leanne and Peter, Barbara and Eleanor's teenagers respectively, had been coming home with similar concerns.

Lois was the only one knitting as the wives discussed the things that'd been happening to them, all of them producing the journals they'd been writing in for reference. Lois shuddered at talk of misplaced tools, moving flowers, colour changing clothing…it seemed to be getting worse. At least none of it was affecting *her*—

Wait.

"What if nothing happening to me…means it'll be worse when it does?" She asked quietly, but it happened to be in the lull of a conversation. A fluttering of pages and all eyes turned to her, but she was staring blankly down at her half— finished blanket.

"Lois, even if that's the case, we'll help you through it." Nancy didn't bother with halfhearted assurances that this wouldn't happen. She knew as well as the others that it was getting worse, so it followed that it'd be worse for Lois than it would be for them at the start.

Lois gave her a weak smile and a nod, busying herself with her knitting again. Nancy frowned. She opened her mouth to say something but decided against it.

Chapter 9

The meeting went on until 9:50 as usual, everyone packing up and leaving after a reminder that their next meeting was the very next day at Barbara's house. Lois was the first one out, arriving back at her house at 10:00 exactly.

"Hello, my love." Paul had waited near the door. Lois put the knitting bag down and forced a smile onto her face. She *was* relieved to see him, though that didn't outweigh the worries that were plaguing her.

"Hello, dearest. I finished another blanket."

Paul smiled as she removed it from the bag.

"When I go out I'll have to purchase more yarn. I'm running low. Been making too many of these, I suppose."

Paul simply nodded.

"I've got the budget for you too, dear, so you know what to take from the general store." She put the knitting bag away before leading him into the guest room turned office that they used for paperwork when nobody was staying over. Lois pulled the budget from the top of the desk, turning on the light so he could go over it. His eyebrows raised slightly at the level of detail in it—excessive, even for Lois.

"Well, this looks all good. I'll copy it down and bring it with me to the store so I'll know what to buy when."

"I already made a copy for you."

He blinked.

"You can take that one, they're functionally identical," she clarified, and he slowly nodded before folding up the paper and putting it into his wallet. He wasn't entirely sure why having already copied it out bothered him so much; usually he'd be thankful for the many conveniences Lois's thoroughness provided.

Right now, though?

Right now, it felt like she was distracting herself.

Paul sighed and pulled her into his arms, kissing the top of her head once she got over her mild surprise at the gesture and wrapped her arms around him. When her fingers dug into his shirt and her grip tightened a little he closed his eyes and tried not to react.

Alright, so she didn't want to talk about it—that didn't mean he couldn't still help. He resolved to call his brother and Winston tomorrow in order to try and get as much information on the case as possible. Lois always wanted to know everything; if he could give her regular updates, maybe it would ease her worries.

He held her for quite a while, expecting her to step away at some point. When she didn't, he eventually pulled back enough to see her face, leaning down and kissing her. At her little hum he, in a fluid motion, bent down and lifted her up into his arms.

"Oh!" she exclaimed, but was cut off by the reconnection of lips. Paul carried her upstairs and into their bedroom, managing to close the door with his foot before walking over and settling onto the bed itself. Lois remained in his lap even after they'd pulled back, nuzzling her face into his neck and sighing warmly.

At least he could help a little.

Lois only broke away from him when she realised it was time to get changed and go to bed. She pulled on a nightgown and washed off all of her makeup, feeling a little better despite her unsolved concerns. Even if she couldn't tell him what was happening, her husband knew that something was wrong—and he knew exactly how to make her feel better.

She smiled, even as she climbed back into bed with a freshly-changed Paul and settled down to sleep. Maybe this would be alright.

Lois woke up at 5:00, rising and getting ready by 5:30. She headed downstairs and prepared Thursday's breakfast before checking the house over for any changes. None. Nothing had moved and nothing was missing. Lois decided to take comfort in this, ignoring the feeling of dread as she went back into the kitchen.

Whether she'd rushed or started too early, Lois had a span of twenty minutes with nothing to do before the girls rose at 6:30. Keeping the food warm, she went to the living room bookcase. Running a finger over the spines, she pulled out a paperback she hadn't yet read. Turning it over in her hands, she read the title aloud: *Tell Me What You Say.*

A manicured eyebrow raised at the cover, which depicted a concerned woman staring at a mirror. Nothing but her face was reflecting in the mirror, but there was something shadowy over her shoulder. Lois gave a short shrug and a small "Hmm," carrying the book with her into the kitchen, sitting down in her chair to read some of it before the kids woke.

Mary bounded down the stairs just as Lois put a napkin in the book to use as a bookmark.

"Morning, mommy!"

"Good morning, sweetheart."

Lois got up, catching Mary before the little girl could sit down and kissing her on the cheek. Mary wrapped her arms around her mother and gave her a squeeze just as Linda descended the stairs.

"Good morning, sweetheart," Lois repeated as Mary let go and jumped into her chair, allowing Lois to give Linda a hug. Linda leaned against her for a few moments, yawning and wishing that she was still in bed.

"Morning, mom," Linda murmured, and Lois gave her a kiss on the forehead before letting her sit down.

"What's school going to be like today?"

"More multiplication!" Mary exclaimed as Lois served them Thursday's breakfast of eggs a la queen, fresh pineapple chunks, fried ham, and toast separate from the eggs. Mary carefully picked out all the walnuts from the eggs as she told her mother all about how easy multiplying was and how she could do it fast because she didn't have to write it out like most of the other kids did. The only lull in the conversation came when Mary began to down her orange juice, at which point Lois turned pointedly to Linda.

"The editing went well. Today we're going to be analyzing published stories the teacher picks and marking those up with our own suggested edits. She says sometimes even published stories still need edits," Linda said, ignoring Mary's exaggerated "Ahh!" upon finishing her glass. Lois poured her more out of the flask on the table and she gave it another sip before digging into her food again.

"I'm glad the editing went well, dear. I'm sure your story was phenomenal. Whenever your teacher calls me she tells me all about how well your writing is going."

Linda blushed warmly, saved from further adoration by Mary suddenly getting up.

"Mary, get your school clothes on, make your bed, and get ready for school, darling."

Mary nodded as she took off upstairs.

"Whenever you're ready, Linda, please do the same." Linda nodded as Lois picked up the used dishware and pulled on her gloves, starting on washing them as her oldest daughter ate in silence.

"What's that?" Linda asked, and Lois turned to see her pointing at the paperback book near Lois's place at the table.

"Oh, that's just a book I pulled from the shelf, dear. Haven't read through it yet."

"What's it about?"

Lois paused to consider the question.

"Well, so far, not much has happened to the main character at all. I'm not very far in. But there are a few strange things happening. I think it's a mystery type book."

Linda nodded, accepting the answer. Lois turned back to continue washing and it wasn't long before her daughter put her dishes in the sink and disappeared upstairs to get ready to leave. Lois managed to scrub everything fairly quickly—she might have been in a rush, but she was too caught up in her thoughts to really notice—so she'd gone back to the book and managed to read another few pages before Mary came running back downstairs.

Before Lois knew it she was waiting on the front porch with Mary and Linda, keeping an eye out for Harold. Lois was holding both girls' hands, grateful Linda hadn't tried to get out of it. Lois's foot tapped impatiently as she watched for

Harold; if she didn't have such a keen sense of the time she would have worried that he was late.

Lois started walking the kids off the porch a microsecond before Harold's car came into view, meeting at the sidewalk at the same time. Harold was shaking his head in mild awe as Lois kissed her daughters goodbye and helped them into the car.

"Lois?" Harold asked before she could start back towards her house, and Lois turned to him.

"Yes, Harold?"

"I'd like to talk with you around lunchtime." The kids' conversations all stopped short and he hastily added, "About flowers."

"Sure, Harold." Lois smiled, having been wanting to talk with him since she'd talked to Daniel. She couldn't let him know straight up what she knew—they had all agreed not to tell their husbands, after all, and Harold was Patricia's husband, so he counted—but it'd be very reassuring to hear someone who didn't spend all their time in a house say they believed that something more was at play than some particularly sneaky hooligans.

Lois waved as Harold drove off, turning and taking the newspaper as she walked back inside. Putting it next to Paul's place like always, she walked upstairs with a smile on her face.

Paul woke up to Lois humming and pressing kisses to his face, her fingers gently massaging into his shoulders. He gave a warm sigh and enjoyed it for a few seconds before reaching up and pulling her over to him, laughing softly as she gave an "Oh!" and landed on his chest.

"Good morning, my dearest," she greeted, smiling as he kissed her properly.

"Good morning, my love," he replied, voice low with sleep. Lois kissed him again, raising a hand to cradle his cheek. He smiled and pulled her closer to him, almost distracting her from the fact that his alarm was about to go off.

Lois pulled away from him a second before it rang, not

needing to look over as she reached to turn it off.

"I'll see you in a few minutes, dear," she murmured, kissing him chastely before getting up and strolling out of the room. She fixed her hair and lipstick in the downstairs bathroom before cooking up his breakfast and starting the coffee. He appeared just as she was pouring it into his cup. He smiled as he walked over and took it with a kiss, sitting down as she was putting breakfast onto a plate. She smiled as she heard him start humming.

"It smells good, love."

He took the newspaper and scanned it over without any audible comments. Lois served herself and sat down across from him, eating in comfortable silence.

"How were Linda and Mary?"

"Mary is excited for more math. Linda's too tired in the mornings to tell, but they're working on improving their editing skills before they write more stories. I think she'll be happy."

He smiled.

"What are you up to today?"

Paul reached over and took one of her hands. She intertwined her fingers with his and tilted her head slightly to the side.

"There's a knitting club meeting today, over at Barbara's."

He nodded. Once he finished his breakfast Lois, who had already finished hers, cleared the table, putting the dishes into the sink to soak. Then, having an idea, she hurried off to the garage—Lois opened the garage door for the car and tucked into her front yard, picking the first morning glory that really caught her eye. She came back into the house to find that Paul had already gotten his shoes and coat on, catching him just as he was reaching for his keys.

He chuckled and bent down a little upon her presenting the flower, allowing her to braid the stem into his locks and tuck it securely behind his ear. He took his keys and put his arm around her, kissing the side of her head. They walked together to the car, Lois leaning on the open window as he sat down and started the engine.

"Have a good day at work, my dearest." She purred, grinning when he leaned up and kissed her on the cheek.

"Have a good day, love."

"Goodbye!" She called as he pulled out of the garage, watching his car disappear down the street. She smiled to herself and started on her chores with a spring in her step, singing to herself all through her cleaning, organising, and exercising. It was as if no time passed at all before a knock on her door and a glance at the clock made her realise it was noon.

She straightened her clothing and opened the front door to find Harold. A small smile formed on her face, but his expression was unreadable.

"Ah, good afternoon, Harry. Come in, come in."

Lois hovered almost anxiously as he removed his dirty work boots and left them on the porch, concern forming in his knitting eyebrows at her movements. He followed her inside, letting her sit him down at the kitchen table. She poured water into a pot and started on tea, pulling out the exact combination of sugar, spices, and honey additions that Harold liked.

"So, what did you want to talk about?" Lois asked once they were seated with their cups and saucers. Her hands shook slightly and anticipation glittered behind her calm expression, steeling internally when she realised he had noticed.

"Danny and I were talking, and he mentioned saying something to you about what's happening around town." Harold said calmly, taking a sip of tea so he could politely pretend to ignore Lois's momentary lapse in expression. She knew he'd seen it, but she appreciated the gesture.

"Oh?"

"Yes. Something's happening in Rose Park, but nobody's talking about it. Patricia apparently told the kids she doesn't believe it's something beyond us."

Harold glanced around the room lightly, as if he was admiring the scenery.

"Nothing's happened here yet."

Lois paled. "No. Nothing has."

Harold nodded, leaning forwards.

"You know it's something more than a person." A statement not a question. She tilted her head to the side, but he nodded as if she'd agreed with him.

"No one person could do this. Not even several people. The keenest of criminals couldn't break into a house without any evidence, especially not to gather every sock and put them in a ball in the closet, or to steal sugar whenever someone's not looking. It's happened so many times, to so many people, all at once. Someone would see something if there was something to see."

Lois was silent, but Harold carried on without seeming to mind.

"No, it's something else. You can feel it, even if you're not paying attention to it. It's like a sense of dread or worry. Everyone's anxious now. It's not just because of things happening—men come by the shop to have their cars looked at and they're worried about this or that. More so than usual. And I know half of them wouldn't know if they walked into the house and it'd been painted red, and none of them believe their wives telling them that something strange is happening. It's not the things that are bothering them, it's what's causing it. It's affecting all of us."

Harold put a hand on Lois's shoulder, gazing intently at the expression on her face.

"Patricia doesn't have to tell me for me to know she thinks it's something more. She won't talk about it because she said she wouldn't to you all in the club. And I know that's why you haven't said anything."

"It's not that," Lois blurted out, surprising herself. She put a hand over her mouth, but as Harold looked at her understandingly and patted her shoulder she gave a sigh and dropped it.

"Well. It's not *just* that," she admitted quietly, "It's that it's so unbelievable. The modern man isn't supposed to believe in ghosts or demons in the home. It's insane, listening to what's happening—things moving, disappearing, appearing where they can't be. Shoes and sugar and socks and jackets. Small things. And their husbands weren't noticing a thing.

77

Why would he believe her? Any of them? They don't know what it's like being in the house all day. When I was younger, I was out a lot and I wouldn't know if something was out of place when I got back. Mother would, but I wouldn't. And it's the same now. He's out of the house all day. He wouldn't know. Why would he believe me? Why would he believe something so inconceivable?"

She was shaking a little now, trying very hard to stay composed. Harold took both of her hands in his, waiting until she felt stable enough to look him in the eye.

"You're right. He won't believe you."

Lois blinked and found herself in her bedroom, in the dark. A glance at the clock told her it was 5:00 AM. She furrowed her eyebrows. That couldn't have been a dream, could it? It was too real…but what else could it have been? She couldn't remember waking up, but her concerns about that melted away as she shook her head and got ready for the day again.

Chapter 10

Lois headed downstairs at 5:30, gaze raking the rooms as she went into the kitchen and started the preparations for Thursday's breakfast.

Once everything was ready to be cooked Lois found herself unable to resist retracing her steps.

Silverware–check.

Plates–check.

Furniture–check.

She went over everything in her mind as she slowly prowled her home, peeking into the bathroom and under the upholstery. She scanned her decorations, the interior of the closets and fridges, her bookshelf–

Lois froze.

Slowly stepping backwards, Lois forced her gaze back to the shelf. A quick count told her that there was a book missing. Bending down to her knees she ran a fingertip over their spines, swallowing hard.

Every book was accounted for except for the one she'd started to read in her dream–*Tell Me What You Say*. A sick feeling formed in her stomach as she pulled books out, trying to see if it'd been tucked behind any of them. Within a minute she'd ripped every book out of the shelf, frantically pawing through them for the volume she'd had.

She shook as she stared at the mess she'd made, breathing rough. Lois forced herself to put them back in the proper order, explanations running through her head. The girls might have taken it, or maybe Paul had taken it for reading material and she'd simply dreamt that it was still there.

Lois paused. The book had been about strange things happening. She closed her eyes to recall its plot–the main character was witnessing the aftermath of odd occurrences, a mystery unravelling in the question of what was causing them.

There was a pause, and then Lois started to laugh. She laughed and laughed and kept laughing, tears running down her face as she grew hysterical. It took her a minute to calm herself down, the thought eventually occurring to her that she might wake another member of the household.

"It was only a dream," she murmured to herself, getting up and going into the bathroom to fix her makeup.

"I dreamt it up. It's like what's happening to me. I was just dreaming. It was only a dream."

She smiled at her reflection once her makeup was ready. Everything was alright–if anything, that proved that the whole ordeal had just been a dream.

Unable to help herself, Lois threw a glance over her shoulder.

Nothing.

Mary bounded down the stairs just as Lois had started to plate breakfast.

"Morning, mommy!"

"Good morning, sweetheart."

Lois got up, catching Mary before the little girl could sit down and kissing her on the cheek. Mary wrapped her arms around her mother and gave her a squeeze just as Linda descended the stairs.

"Good morning, sweetheart," Lois repeated as Mary let go and jumped into her chair, allowing Lois to give Linda a hug. Linda leaned against her for a few moments, yawning and wishing that she was still in bed.

"Morning, mom," Linda murmured, and Lois gave her a kiss on the forehead before letting her sit down.

"What's school going to be like today?"

"More multiplication!" Mary exclaimed as Lois served them Thursday's breakfast. Lois had a sense of déjà vu as Mary carefully picked out all the walnuts from the eggs, telling her mother all about how easy multiplying was and how she could do it fast because she didn't have to write it out like most of the other kids did. It was exactly what she'd said in the dream. Lois swallowed hard and reasoned that she was just good at predicting her daughter.

The only lull in the conversation came when Mary began to down her orange juice, at which point Lois turned pointedly to Linda.

"The editing went well. Today we're going to be analyzing published stories the teacher picks and marking those up with our own suggested edits. She says sometimes even published stories still need edits," Linda said, ignoring Mary's exaggerated "Ahh!" upon finishing her glass. Lois poured her more out of the flask on the table, hand shaking slightly at the repeated words, and Mary gave it another sip before digging into her food again.

"I'm glad the editing went well, dear. I'm sure your story was phenomenal. Whenever your teacher calls me she tells me all about how well your writing is going," Lois repeated from memory. Linda blushed warmly, saved from further adoration by Mary suddenly getting up.

"Mary, get your school clothes on, make your bed, and get ready for school, darling."

Mary nodded as she took off upstairs.

"Whenever you're ready, Linda, please do the same." Linda nodded as Lois picked up the used dishware and pulled on her gloves, starting on washing them as her oldest daughter ate in silence. Now that she wasn't facing either of the children, she allowed her expression to falter. It was happening exactly the same way—what a detailed dream!

It wasn't long before Linda put her dishes in the sink and disappeared upstairs to get ready to leave. Lois took her time washing them, finishing just moments before Mary came running back downstairs. As if in a trance, she helped them with their bags and gave them their lunches in exactly the same way. Walking out onto the front porch, she was hit with the scent of her morning glories, reminding her of what she was going to give Paul later.

Lois kept an eye out for Harold. Holding both girls' hands, again, she gazed serenely at the street, knowing exactly when he was going to come—even more exactly than usual.

Lois started walking the kids off the porch at the same second Harold's car came into view, meeting at the sidewalk at the same time. Harold was shaking his head in mild awe as Lois kissed her daughters goodbye and helped them into the car.

"Lois?" Harold asked before she could start back towards her house, and Lois turned to him. Her expression must have shocked him, some of it registering in his eyes.

"Yes, Harold?"

He swallowed a statement, which she expected she already knew. Things were diverging.

"Tell Paul I'd like to talk with him. I'll be dropping around at his work at some point."

"Sure, Harold," Lois said with a false smile, having a feeling that she knew what he wanted to stay.

Lois waved as Harold drove off, turning and taking the newspaper as she walked back inside. Putting it next to Paul's place like always, she put smile on her face. At least her dream's way of waking him up had been unusually pleasant; no reason not to do that again.

Paul woke up to Lois humming and pressing kisses to his face, her fingers gently massaging into his shoulders. He gave a warm sigh and enjoyed it for a few seconds before reaching up and pulling her over to him, laughing softly as she gave an "Oh!" and landed on his chest.

"Good morning, my dearest," she greeted, smiling as he kissed her properly.

"Good morning, my love," he replied, voice low with sleep. Lois kissed him again, surprising him slightly at how romantic she was feeling that morning. One of her hands rose up and cradled his cheek as he pulled her a little closer to him, a smile forming on his face. She always knew exactly how to bring back the giddiness most couples said ended after the honeymoon.

Lois didn't even pull away from him to reach her hand over and turn his alarm off, lips remaining on his. She only pulled away at the thought that she'd better get breakfast ready.

"I'll see you in a few minutes, dear," she murmured, kissing him chastely before getting up and strolling out of the room.

Paul came downstairs to find Lois pouring his coffee, smiling as he walked over and took it with a kiss. He sat down as she was putting breakfast onto a plate, sniffing the air and humming.

"It smells good, love."

A pause.

"Where's the newspaper?"

Lois straightened.

"What do you mean, it's right—" She stopped mid-sentence upon turning around, staring at the table. The newspaper. She'd put it right by his place like always, but it was gone. Nobody else was in the house. Lois snapped to look out the kitchen window, her eyes widening as she spied the paper on the path up to her house. It hadn't happened like this in the dream.

Like Patricia, Lois.

Lois forced any expression of fear or alarm from her face.

"I must have forgotten to bring it in, dear. Harold stopped to ask me something and I just got distracted, I suppose. I'll go get it."

Paul nodded as he watched her go, his eyes following her as she left the kitchen and listening to her heels click outside. He couldn't remember the last time she forgot the newspaper, if ever. Even when the girls had been babies she'd never gotten so distracted as to forget to bring it in.

"Here you are!" Lois interrupted his thoughts as she held it out to him. There was a smile on her face and he wondered if maybe he was overthinking it as she leaned forwards and kissed him again, going back to the range to finish arranging his breakfast. He'd practically forgotten about the lapse as the food was served, hunger overriding what he'd convinced himself was nothing.

"How were Linda and Mary?" Paul asked as Lois quickly ate.

"Mary is excited for more math. Linda's too tired in the

83

mornings to tell, but they're working on improving their editing skills before they write more stories. I think she'll be happy."

Paul got the strange feeling that he'd had almost this exact conversation with Lois not very long ago. He could never know how much she felt the same way—instead, he brushed it off; most of their mornings consisted of seemingly repeated dialogue.

He smiled.

"What are you up to today?"

Paul reached over and took one of her hands. She intertwined her fingers with his and tilted her head slightly to the side.

"There's a knitting club meeting today, over at Barbara's."

He nodded.

"There seems to be a lot of those lately, aren't there?" Paul asked. He was starting to miss being able to spend the evening relaxing with her.

"I don't think so. Same as usual," Lois lied, putting on a slightly confused expression. Paul shook it off and Lois's other hand gathered into a fist for a moment, guilt seeping into her mind at the falsehood. His focus shifted to the newspaper and she let out a silent breath. His hand gave hers a light squeeze as he picked it up with the other and began to scan over it.

There was an editorial about a wife's specific case of disappearing objects. Hidden within an inner page there was an actual article by his brother James about the rise in reported crime and a lack of police resolution, with a note about how most of the cases ended up solving themselves.

It was small, and Paul found it likely that the editor wasn't willing to let James stir the pot too much; Rose Park was known for being as sweet and safe as the name implied. With a sharp eye, Paul kept going over other editorials, other reports that had been scattered amongst the more normal articles.

Cases still unsolved, more complaints coming in, things going missing more often, stranger occurrences…Paul stopped himself from frowning, worrying how it might affect Lois. As far as he knew, she hadn't been reading the paper lately; usually she'd talk about the articles over dinner during a lull in Mary's conversations. He couldn't take it with him—that she'd notice—but if he didn't bring any attention to it, perhaps he could spare the worry.

At least, until he called his brother and Winston to get the fuller story.

Lois disappeared after putting the dishes in the sink, leaving Paul to get his jacket and shoes on alone. She reappeared as he was going to get his keys from the bowl, holding up a flower with a slightly crooked smile: a blue morning glory from her front garden. The very same one she'd gotten in her dream. It was as beautiful as she'd remembered. He chuckled and bent down as she tucked it behind his ear and braided the stem into his locks, giving him a kiss before he straightened and got his keys.

They walked together to the car, Lois leaning on the open window as he sat down and started the engine. As it made the same sound she had to resist reacting to another wave of déjà vu.

"Have a good day at work, my dearest," she purred, grinning when he leaned up and kissed her on the cheek.

"Have a good day, love."

"Goodbye!" She called as he pulled out of the garage, watching his car disappear down the street. Once he was completely gone and the garage door was closed she let down the act, a few stray tears falling down her face. The dream was still bothering her, but the newspaper was bothering her more. She must have just forgotten to bring it in—she did it every day, it wasn't out of the realm of possibility that she'd just assume she'd done it. Especially after living such a lifelike dream where she had.

Right?

Chapter 11

When Paul arrived at the general store, he was grateful to find that nobody was waiting for him. He opened up and checked the inventory before setting up behind the counter, taking a newspaper and reading it in full. It was clear things were getting worse. There were bigger articles dedicated to it, which he noticed now that he could pull out yesterday's paper and compare. As he actually read through the editorials and his brother's article a pit formed in his stomach. He had to force a smile when someone walked into the store.

It took over two hours for Paul to finally be free to make a phone call—lots of people were coming into the store to pick up various things, many of them re-upping on things he knew they had recently purchased. Some even stopped by twice.

The first person Paul called was James, wanting to be as informed as possible before calling Winston. It didn't take more than two rings for James to pick up.

"James McCarthy, who may I ask is speaking?" he asked in his work voice.

"It's Paul."

"Ah! How are you? You usually don't call me here."

Paul took a deep breath.

"Can you tell me what you know about all these reports of things moving and going missing? Lois is scared to death and I'm not doing so good myself."

James' voice was noticeably quieter as he responded, "Well, I'm not supposed to, but here's what I know. All over Rose Park people have been reporting things going missing— small things, but usually a specific trend. Socks, utensils, food; nothing big. Everyone's only been losing things smaller than a breadbox, and after a few days they find them in some inexplicable place. Other people are having things move around the house; me and Nancy actually were having a problem where jackets kept moving."

"At first, I didn't notice, but after a while I realised Nancy wasn't being crazy. I don't know how it was happening, but they were certainly moving around. The police can't find anything, and I'm starting to think that it must be some real professionals."

Paul was about to say something when James continued, "The thing is, nobody seems to have seen anyone new. There are no strangers in Rose Park. Nobody has seen any evidence of anyone breaking in, and a lot of the cases are…strange. Nancy told me that Barbara found all of her utensils in a locked lockbox that only she had the code for, and when I talked to Winston he mentioned another case like that where things were removed from a lockbox that was secured. Winston was really cagey on details, as usual, but that was enough for me. That, and with how nobody's seen anything…it's really a mystery. I know that probably doesn't help, but that's all I know."

Paul sucked some air in through his teeth.

"Alright. Thanks, James."

"Has anything happened to you?" he asked quickly.

"No."

James sighed. "Oh well. I've got to go, but that's what I know. Bye, Paul."

"Bye, James."

Paul massaged his temples, groaning softly. He had learned absolutely nothing good from that phone call. There was even *less* evidence than he'd originally assumed. His only hope now was to try and get something out of Winston. He dialed up his office number, hoping against hopes that he was there. After three rings Paul was worried he was out on a case, but finally Winston picked up.

"Police Chief's office, this is Chief Johnson speaking."

"It's Paul."

A relieved sigh.

"Oh, thank the stars. Hello, Paul, I was worried you were someone else calling about another missing thing. Everything's getting worse."

Paul stayed silent, allowing Winston to explain, "We're getting inundated with calls. Things are getting stranger, too. Several husbands have called to report that, amoung things going missing, their wives seem to be seeing things. It looks like we've got some kind of hysteria problem, people hallucinating things out of fear. Either that, or these criminals are both incredibly sneaky *and* incredibly bold. A few people reported things like objects changing colour or getting switched out for other things. In their own homes, while they're there."

Massaging the bridge of his nose, Paul gave a grunt.

"Should I even be relieved that nothing's happened to me and Lois yet?"

"Are you sure nothing's happened to her?"

Paul scoffed.

"Don't write me off just yet. I know things are already happening in my house, but I only heard about the last few things from Jules or May mentioning them on the side. I know Cynthia's aware of it, but she hasn't been telling me everything unless I ask. And I know she's hearing whatever's going on with the knitting club wives. They're keeping it hush. I know they probably don't think anyone's going to believe them—if they've started seeing things, I can see their concerns—but it might start hindering my case..."

"Lois would tell me if anything was wrong," Paul insisted, even as doubt formed in his chest. He knew she was hiding some things from him. Maybe it wasn't just a reluctance to complain—what if something had happened in their house and she hadn't told him? What if the love of his life didn't feel safe in her own home, with her own husband?

"I don't know Lois as well as you do, but I get the feeling it'd hurt her more for you not to believe her than to not tell you something crazy. And with them likely thinking this is something supernatural like Harold, I can see why she'd refrain."

Paul muttered out a string of curses, at which point Winston laughed.

"Lois trusts me. And I trust her."

"Lois has a very good head on her shoulders. Anyone that organised has to be sensible. If your wife hasn't told you anything, it probably means that nothing's happened to her," he conceded, but he'd already planted seeds of doubt and worry in Paul's mind.

"So, maybe for some reason you aren't being targeted. Or, maybe, she hasn't noticed."

"She'd notice," Paul said immediately. Winston grunted.

"As much as it pains me, you're right. Lois would notice. But it doesn't make any sense why nothing's happened to her. I don't understand why they wouldn't target your house when they've targeted all the houses around you. There's no sense to it! But maybe that's the point…"

Winston began muttering something to himself, but Paul was too concerned with the implications of his statements to hear. Either Lois was hiding something from him—something he *knew* was happening, though he hoped not for something this serious—or, for some unknown reason, whatever was going on wasn't happening to them specifically. At least, not yet.

"Maybe Harold is on to something," Paul said, the words bitter in his mouth.

"Oh, come on, think reasonably, Paul. The supernatural doesn't exist."

Paul clicked his tongue. It was a terrifying thought.

"No, you're right. Probably not."

"*Definitely* not."

In another situation Paul would have laughed at Winston's conviction.

"Look, I've got to go, but keep an eye out, Paul. If anything happens to you two at all, I want to know immediately. Any little detail might help me understand why you were targeted late, or even help solve the case."

"Alright. Okay. Thanks, Winston. Goodbye."

"Goodbye."

Paul hung up and held his face in his hands, having difficulty slapping a smile on the next time a customer walked through the door. They didn't notice. It was another housewife, buying another supply of something he knew she'd already bought recently. They paid without looking him in the eye, hurrying out back to their car. Back to the house they were terrified to leave, worried something more would go missing in the short time they were gone.

"Lois must be terrified." He murmured, staring at the clock and groaning when he saw it was only noon. He couldn't go home early again—she'd have his head, scared or not—so he'd have to deal with his emotions for now. If she got especially worried, she'd call. Or at least, he hoped she would.

Paul was saved from his worries when the door opened and he turned to see Harold, who again came right over to the counter without any intention of buying anything. He smiled, somewhere caught between relieved and worried. The conflict must have been clear on his face, because Harold put a hand on his shoulder and patted it a few times before talking.

"Something's happened to Lois."

Paul's breath hitched, he paled, and Harold squeezed his shoulder.

"She didn't tell me about it, before you ask." Harold added quickly, but this did not dispel the quiet horror on Paul's face.

"What happened?"

"I'm not sure. But I know it was something. She started walking off the steps the moment her house came into view when I drove over to pick up the girls, meeting me at the sidewalk instead of waiting on the porch like usual. I got her attention and she turned to me with this *look* on her face. Wasn't sure what to say, honestly. But I know something happened. There was this bad energy around her, too. Worse than when things happen in my house."

Paul chose to ignore this last part, having enough to deal with from the fact that the look on Lois's face had somehow stunned Harold into silence. Harold was rarely surprised by anything, let alone other people's facial expressions.

"What do you *think* happened?" Paul clarified, wanting some kind of answer beyond 'something.' 'Something' was enough to make him close up shop right then and there and run home.

"Must've been something spooky enough to put her on edge. Maybe she saw something that didn't make sense. Some of the husbands have started complaining about their wives seeing things. Doubt they've all gone off their heads. They're all seeing something. Lois is real logical, it'd definitely freak her out if she saw something she didn't understand."

Paul was silent. Winston and Harold's differing opinion on the same phenomenon aside, Lois 'freaking out' was an understatement. Wherever it was polite, Lois would micromanage. She couldn't help it when she had the time on her hands. If something happened that she *knew* shouldn't have happened...he didn't even want to think about it.

"Are you sure she didn't just have a bad dream or something?" Paul asked miserably.

"I doubt it."

After a heavy sigh, Paul reached for the phone. Harold caught his hand before he could pick up the receiver. He may have been thin, but he was much stronger than he looked—Paul didn't bother trying to push through his grip.

"Paul, what do you want to say to her?" Harold asked pointedly.

"I need to ask her if anything happened."

"If she didn't tell you before, why would she tell you now?"

Paul groaned in frustration.

"My wife needs to feel safe in her own house!" He exclaimed, glad there was nobody else in the store. Harold barely reacted aside from a softening in his gaze.

"Paul," he started gently, "I know you don't believe me about what's happening. So, let's go over this your way. Say there's a bunch of prolific criminal pranksters in Rose Park. Nobody's seen them. Nobody has been able to prevent them from doing anything, not by putting things in lockboxes, not by adding locks to their houses, not by putting powder on the sills. You cannot keep her safe from something you can't stop."

Paul chewed his bottom lip in an attempt to prevent from

91

either shouting or otherwise blurting out with some strong emotion. An irritating pressure began to prick at the corners of his eyes.

"Now, think about this from Lois's point of view. Whether she thinks it's criminals or knows it's something else doesn't matter for right now. What *does* matter is that something happened to her that she doesn't understand. Lois is even more scrupulous than the others, she'd know if anything moved in that house. You could put a book one position over and she'd probably be able to move it back to where she'd had it—even I know how good her memory is."

"Now here lies the problem: Lois also knows how good her memory is. Lois also knows that she knows where everything is. If she encountered something she doesn't understand, a few things will happen: she'll feel like she can't trust herself anymore, she'll question everything that's happening around her, and she won't tell anyone unless she thinks they'll believe her. She needs an anchor, Paul."

Paul opened his mouth to say something but Harold kept going, "And that anchor is the knitting club."

Paul muttered something rather rude under his breath.

"All of them are experiencing the same things while we're off at work, to a degree. All of them are talking about it. And all of them believe each other."

He made sure Paul was looking him in the eye.

"And they *know* it's not some impossibly sneaky villains."

"What is it then, Harold?" Paul demanded a bit loudly. Harold tilted his head slightly, judging Paul's expression.

"As I said before, I don't know everything out there. But I know for an absolute fact that this is some sort of energy, possibly even an entity. I don't have access to the police records to check definitively if it's happened before, but some of the library's old archives mention events very similar to ours of things going missing. They thought it was criminals, just like Winston and most of the town do. But they didn't have a real newspaper then, so there isn't too much information on it. It's happening again. And it's not criminals. Do you really think someone got into your house, through your new locks, without disturbing your sills' powder, just to mess with Lois? Do you *really* think someone or someones are doing that to everyone?"

Paul's expression steeled. He was starting to have his doubts, but the thought of this being some sort of uncontrollable phenomenon that was targeting everyone without reason and without a way to prevent it was terrifying. He wanted to shut it out, to ignore it and be as confident as Winston that it wasn't possible.

But Harold was right. Everything that was happening…it was impossible for a person or people to be doing it. For so long, with no evidence, to so many people?

"I know it's scary," Harold admitted gently. Paul gave him a look, but Harold saw right through it. He sighed.

"Think about it."

He let go of Paul's hand, lacing his fingers together and resting his chin on them. Paul's hand hovered, touched the receiver, and stopped. He thought for a few moments before snatching it up and dialing his home number.

Lois picked up after three rings.

"Hello?"

"Lois, it's me." His tone was slightly defeated, but he made an effort to sound pleasant.

"Oh, good afternoon, love! You never call at work. What is it?"

He winced at the nervousness in her tone she was so obviously trying to suppress.

"I just felt like hearing your voice. Is everything going well at home?"

A pause. That was bad.

"Of course, dear. Why wouldn't it?"

"Oh, just with everything everyone's talking about. I wanted to make sure that nothing has happened to you. I'd hate for you to be worried about anything."

She gave a laugh. A nervous laugh. He shut his eyes tightly.

"No, nothing's happened to me, dear. Everything's where it's supposed to be."

"That's good to hear," he said, forcing his voice to keep calm.

"Well, if that's all, honey, I've got to get back to the garden."

Please tell me what's wrong. "Yes, that's all."

"Alright, Paul, I'll see you in—"

"I just wanted to say that I love you, and that you can tell me anything, alright? Please tell me if anything happens to you. I wouldn't want you to be alone if anything scared you." The quiet desperation in his voice made Harold sigh. It was a few seconds before Lois responded.

"I—yes, I. I would. Of course. I love you too."

There was a click as she hung up. Paul hadn't missed the worry in her voice, the rushing of stumbled words. Harold was right. Something had happened.

Paul replaced the receiver and put his head in his hands.

"Think about it."

He didn't look up as Harold's footsteps receded and the door opened and closed, the little bell signaling to him that he was alone yet again.

Chapter 12

Lois had pushed Paul's call out of her mind by the time the girls arrived home from school. She made them a snack and listened to them talk as she continued preparing fruit cake bars for the knitting club meeting that night.

"Mom?" Linda interrupted Lois's halfhearted reverie, her mother looking up to see Mary had run off to do her homework and left the two alone.

"Yes, dear?"

"I was thinking of going over to see dad. I have quiet work today."

Lois smiled. That would distract him.

"Oh, of course, honey."

Linda nodded, taking up her backpack and walking out of the house. Lois watched her until she disappeared down the street, tabling the dessert making so she could wash the dishes. Mary was playing rock records in the living room, birds were chirping outside, she could faintly smell the perfume of her flowers from the door having been opened…maybe nothing was wrong at all. Maybe it really had been all just a dream.

Paul felt as though he could win an Oscar for his acting chops as he pretended there was nothing wrong in front of his customers. Luckily for him, most of them probably wouldn't have noticed if he was openly sobbing and guzzling a bottle of gin—they were distracted, not making eye contact. The familiar faces of women terrified to talk about what was happening to them, uncomfortable with the concept of small talk lest they say something that reveals them. It was starting to drain him, seeing all of these people in such distress.

His front was put to the test when the door opened and his daughter walked in. Paul swallowed a groan. Linda was observant and perceptive—he'd have to be very careful around her.

"Hello, darling," He greeted as she padded over to him, giving him a smile as she went behind the counter.

"Hi, dad. I have quiet work today."

Paul nodded and watched her go into his small backroom, closing the door behind her. He let out a heavy sigh, unsure of what he'd do if she'd decided to just hang around. Every topic of conversation would be a possible freefall into talking about Lois, how he was worried about Lois, *what's happening with your mother, Linda?*

Paul groaned, checking his watch. 4:03. Time was moving like jelly.

"Paul!"

Paul looked over to see Winston was almost directly in front of him. He must have zoned out—maybe it was closer to 5 o'clock now? He glanced at his watch.

4:08.

"Are you alright?" Winston asked, and Paul looked back over at him.

"Yeah, I just—I'm worried about Lois," he said this last part quietly, gesturing to the back room. Winston was over often enough to know that meant that Linda was doing her homework in the next room.

"For good reason. I need more locks."

Paul got up and showed Winston over to where he kept the locks. He'd just restocked them that morning, but half of them were already gone. Everyone was drilling more and more into every part of their homes that opened. Someone had even asked him how to install extra locks to a garage door without messing with the weight of it.

Winston looked over them, ultimately taking several.

"I already picked up screws from Harold. Told me I'm wasting my time, as always. But I don't know what he expects me to do," Winston explained as they went back to the counter, his foot tapping agitatedly as Paul told him his amount and filled out the receipt.

"I don't understand how this is happening. I'm at the station real early in the morning every day now. I sleep there some nights. I can't get any cracks in the case. I have the boys on patrol all the time. Nobody sees anything. Nobody's reporting anything except more and more things going missing, more and more things changing places, more and more things changing colour or whatever. It's driving me mad. These people mean business." He kept his voice low for Linda's sake as he prattled on, handing Paul a wad of cash. Paul took the proper amount and handed him back the rest, which he shoved roughly into his pocket.

"Harold came to see me today."

Winston froze in place.

"What'd he say?"

"I'm starting to think he's right, Winston."

Winston didn't sneer at the suggestion like he normally would have, though his expression was guarded.

"What did he say, Paul?"

"He said that it wasn't possible for human beings to be doing this to so many people all at once without leaving any evidence or being seen. And I think he's right." It was obvious from Paul's tone that he was the very opposite of happy about this, troubled even. Winston found this fearful resignation to be almost as convincing as the statement itself.

"I—"

"I know you don't want to believe it, Winston," Paul interrupted before he could give a flimsy excuse, "But at the very least, could you talk with Harold about it seriously? He said he was going through old news records but couldn't access other ones. If you both look over all the information, maybe you'll both come to a satisfactory conclusion."

Silence.

"Winston, I need this solved. It's starting to affect Lois."

"Alright. I'll work with him. If we find anything I'll tell you." Winston nodded.

Paul gave him a shaky smile and Winston took his locks in a paper bag, gait a bit shaky as he left the store. Paul glanced down at his watch.

4:18.

He let his head hit the counter with a thud, listening to the ticking of his watch as the seconds meandered by.

Lois was nearly finished with dinner when Paul came into the room, clearly in a bit of a rush—Linda hadn't even managed to leave the garage yet.

"Are you alright?" Lois asked as he hurried over and wrapped his arms around her, giving her a squeeze and rocking her side to side. Lois, surprised at the gesture, took a few seconds to return the hug.

"Hi…mom…" Linda said when she came in, clearly curious of the scene that had unfolded. Her father had bolted out of the car like his life depended on it, leaving her to close the garage door and make sure the car was locked. Something had worried him; she assumed it had something to do with the conversation he'd had with Winston earlier. She'd not been able to make out what the police chief had said, but it had been a quiet and illegally quick ride home.

"Hello, darling," Lois replied, voice slightly cut off due to Paul's grip. Linda stared for a few moments before shrugging and heading up to her room.

"Paul, what's got you all riled up like this?" Lois asked once Linda was out of an earshot, Paul had taken to showering her in kisses and it took a moment for him to pull back, face her, and respond.

"I just needed to see you."

Lois was concerned by the way he'd said that.

"Did Harold say something to you?"

He froze.

"Why do you ask?"

"He said he wanted to talk to you this morning."

It took a few moments for Paul to decide what to say—he didn't want a repeat of his first phone call to her where she'd insisted nothing was wrong. He'd ease into it, wait for her to come to him.

"Yes, we were just talking about what was happening around town. What it could be. Harold has some…interesting ideas."

Lois's eyes widened slightly, emotion flashing in her eyes

for less than a second. She opened her mouth, eyebrows knitting slightly as she licked her lips. She wanted to say something. She wanted to tell him.

"I have to take the ham loaf out before it burns."

Cynthia's words kept her mouth shut.

Paul hovered closely as Lois finished dinner—an arm around her, a head on her shoulder, a hand on her arm, a kiss on her cheek—she wasn't sure whether to enjoy or be concerned by all the attention. Whatever Harold had said clearly made an impression.

Mary talked all through dinner, Linda making a very strong effort to act like nothing was wrong as she engaged her. Every time Paul looked like he might say something Lois would find a way to keep Mary talking, even turning to Linda when her youngest got too distracted by eating. Paul took her hand and squeezed it a few times, but she didn't give in until Linda and Mary had finished eating and left the kitchen.

She stood up and swept all the dishes into the sink, Paul reaching out and stopping her before she could start washing them.

"Lois," he pleaded, taking both her hands in his and turning her so she'd face him. Her expression was the picture of mild confusion and curiosity, almost entirely obscuring any worry. It was as if he'd dreamt the whole day—but those endless seconds were far too real to have been imagined.

"Yes, my dearest?"

"I love you. You know that, yeah?"

She blinked.

"Of course I know that. I love you too."

He nodded, pulling her into a hug. This one felt more intimate than his desperate grasp earlier; he cradled her head, nuzzling into her and softly kissing her hair as she wrapped her arms around him. She sighed gently and her fingers curled into his shirt, breathing slow and almost imperceptibly shaky.

Almost.

It was difficult for Paul not to ask her to stay as she gathered her knitting club materials and put the fruit cake bars into her dessert tin. He settled instead to kiss her at the door, a romantic affair that *almost* had her second guessing her decision. But, club supplies in hand, she was off to Barbara's house as Paul stood on the porch and wished he knew what to say.

Chapter 13

Lois had raised her hand to knock but hadn't yet made contact with the door when she heard shouting from inside. At first it was indecipherable, and she leaned in to hear.

"I *told* you not to touch my things!"

"I didn't, Richard, it was—"

"I don't want to hear a damn word out of you about things moving or being stolen! Nobody's been in our house, I've checked the locks myself! You've lost your goddamn mind! I ought to get you institutionalised!"

Lois winced.

"Richard, I, I—"

"If you start crying I'll make you stop."

The conversation got too quiet to hear before a slamming door made Lois jump. She heard the stomping of feet, the almost demonic screech of the garage door being yanked up faster than it should have, and the sound of the car being started. She watched as Richard sped out of the lot and in the direction of the town. There were a few seconds of silence before Lois gently knocked on the door.

Sometimes, being early was not a good thing. Barbara opened the door on the very verge of tears, her hands shaking. She couldn't even muster up a false smile.

"How long have you been there?" She whispered. Lois her things down right on the porch and wrapped her arms around Barbara, who held onto her tightly and started to sob. Lois stared blankly forwards as she murmured assurances to her friend.

Would Paul act like this?

Lois had calmed Barbara down and helped her fix her makeup before the next person, Cynthia, arrived. Lois was in the kitchen warming the knitting club treats up for Barbara as the latter sat in the living room knitting. Cynthia said hello to

Barbara before stopping in the kitchen, throwing a glance in the direction of the doorway when Lois turned to her.

"Richard was yelling at her," Lois explained very quietly.

Cynthia put a hand over her mouth.

"The poor dear."

"It was awful," Lois practically whispered, and Cynthia's eyebrows furrowed.

"You heard it?"

"I came a little too early today, it would seem."

Cynthia shook her head.

"They can't accept it. It's too out there." She popped her chess pie into the oven with Lois's dessert.

Lois nodded numbly, giving a sigh. The doorbell rang before Cynthia could say anything about Paul, both of them looking in the direction of the door.

"I'll get it," Cynthia said, and she left Lois alone with her thoughts.

The club meeting was, overall, very similar to the last one. Everyone was reporting things moving, going missing, seeing unusual things—it had gotten more frequent, but in the grand scheme of things nothing had changed.

"I found the book I'd seen the word 'Eldritch' in before," Patricia announced during a lull in the conversation, "We had it in the recesses of the house. Harry must have gotten it at some point."

She pulled a worn leather book from her purse.

"*Beyond the Wall of Sleep* by H.P. Lovecraft. A storybook?"

"It is fictional, but the creatures in his stories bear a lot of resemblance to what's happening to us. Impossible cities, unknowable creatures, small things happening that are only noticed by a minority of people, minor things happening over a period of time. It's uncanny."

The wives leaned in as Patricia briefly summarised "The Call of Cthulhu" and a few other stories.

"Well, like it says. I guess we can't really do anything. If it's really something so vast and great...we have no control at all..." Eleanor murmured.

102

Again, such a bleak statement the room devolved into different conversations. It didn't take long for the wives to delve into the delicate territory of free will, inevitability, and hopelessness in the face of nature. Lois kept quiet as the women discussed whether anything they were doing ultimately had any meaning at all.

"Has anything happened to you yet, Lois?"

Lois briefly considered the newspaper incident before deciding it must have been her mistake.

"No, I don't think so."

Lois finished two blankets that meeting. It was easy to focus on it when she didn't have any worrying events of her own to recount—the lack of control in their situation and Richard's reaction to being told inconceivable things were happening was concerning, but she felt like she at least had the togetherness of club. They all would believe her if something happened, and that was enough.

Well. Enough that she didn't feel a painful ache not telling Paul about it.

He was waiting for her when she came home that night, unusually tired as she put away her things. He'd already changed into his pyjamas, taking her hand and quietly leading her upstairs once she was ready for bed. He didn't say anything as she changed, taking her in his arms once she'd climbed into bed. Paul held her as if she was a precious, fleeting entity, worried that she'd disappear if he let go. Lois nuzzled into him as he cradled her, falling asleep fairly quickly.

It took almost an hour for Paul to fall asleep, but his wife's gentle breathing settled him into a dreamless slumber.

Lois opened her eyes to see it was still dark. She looked over at the clock, but it was impossible to read, as if the radium paint's glow had faded. Lois easily pulled herself out of Paul's limp grip, fully aware that there was no point in trying to lie back down. After getting ready in the bathroom she padded downstairs and into the kitchen, making herself some coffee she didn't need before searching the house for anything out of place.

Nothing.

She wasn't sure how long she was awake before her internal clock informed her that it was time to make breakfast for the kids. Friday's schedule dictated sunny side up eggs, cereal, toast with jam, pineapple chunks, and fried ham. She'd served everything onto their plates when Mary and Linda came down.

"Good morning!" Linda called.

"Good morning, sweetheart," Lois greeted pleasantly. She was a little surprised that Mary wasn't up for conversation and Linda was, but with all the excitement of the past week it wasn't a big shock.

They ate breakfast in silence, Lois feeling the need to make conversation.

"So, what are you doing in school today?"

"More reading," Linda offered, and Lois nodded before turning to Mary. Mary yawned.

"Are you alright, honey?"

Mary nodded.

"We're reading our stories to the class today. I hope everyone likes mine," Linda said, her voice strangely energetic.

"Oh, how exciting! I'm sure they will." Lois grinned, and Linda copied the expression.

Lois gathered their dishes once they were done and was about to send them up to make their beds when she paused. An uneasy feeling pressed against her chest. She wasn't sure what it was, but...

"Linda?"

"Yes, mommy?"

Lois winced ever so slightly.

"Didn't you already read your stories out to the class?"

Mary and Linda both stared up at her.

"These are new stories. We just wrote them."

Lois closed her eyes.

"Of course. Could you remind me of what the last story was about?"

"Yes, mommy. It was about a policeman going back in

104

time to the old west."

Lois sighed deeply, her breath shaking.

"No, it wasn't. You wrote that last year. Your last story was about an alien blending into an Earth neighborhood."

Lois opened her eyes to see her children were gone. Her heart dropped in her chest and she checked the whole first floor before bolting up the stairs, bursting into Linda's bedroom. Empty. She ran into Mary's—empty. Lois's entire body was shaking as she ran between both rooms, checking the sills for any movement in the powder. None.

Too quick to avoid banging into a wall or two, Lois ran into her bedroom to wake up Paul. It took what felt like hours to shake him out of his sleep.

"What?" He asked, not bothering to sit up.

"They're gone."

"What?"

"They're *gone*, Paul. Our—our daughters. They're. They're gone! They're gone, they, there's nothing, they're just—Paul. Mary and Linda, they, they—"

Paul sat up and slapped her across the face to stop her from babbling. She froze, a few tears trailing down her cheeks.

"What happened?"

"They're gone," she whispered, her voice shaking.

"What did you do?"

"W—what?"

"What. Did. You. Do?"

She blinked.

"I—I didn't do anything, I, I went downstairs and made breakfast, and, and they came down, but they were acting strange. And I closed my eyes and when I opened them they, they were *gone*, and I went upstairs, and their rooms are empty, and—"

She gasped and stopped talking when Paul raised his hand again, clearly willing to slap her out of another bout of hysterics. Lois stood up and backed away a step.

"Where are you going?" he demanded, and she shook her head.

"You're not Paul," she whispered.

"Don't be stupid," he snapped, but she turned and ran out of the room. She tripped and fell down the stairs—bouncing off the landing and into the living room, too shocked to cry at the pain. A prolific bruise formed on one of her legs, but she couldn't care less as she stood up and hurried for the door. Lois was about to reach it when Paul stepped out of nowhere, stopping her as she gasped.

"Lois, what's wrong? What is it?" he asked, voice soft and pleading. He put his hands on her shoulders and she let her muscles relax.

"P—Paul?" she stammered, and he nodded, a look of concern growing on his face. Lois sobbed, wrapping her arms around him.

"The—the kids, are, are *gone*, and you, you were, but it wasn't you, I don't, I don't know, I don't…"

Paul kissed the top of her head and cradled her head against him, the other arm keeping a tight grip around her.

"It's alright. It's alright. Everything is okay."

After a while, Paul started to hum to calm her down, and soon after she began to grow quieter.

The safe feeling she'd gotten the minute he wrapped his arms around her began to fade when she realised what he was singing. *Little White Lies* had never been Lois's favourite, and Paul knew it.

She sniffed.

"Could you hum our song?"

"Of course," he murmured in that soft, warm voice, and he started off…into *Happy Days Are Here Again.* Lois's blood went cold—she tried to pull away from him, but his grip was like iron.

"Honey?"

No reply. Lois kept trying to rip herself out of his grip, but she couldn't get free.

"Let me go!" she shouted, kicking and hitting anything she could touch, but with no give.

Lois woke up with a gasp, ripping herself out of Paul's grasp as she sat up.

"Lois?"

106

Lois gave another gasp and tumbled back, nearly falling off the bed.

"Lois! What's wrong? What's the matter?" He asked, but she winced when he reached for her.

Eyes wide, Paul froze; she'd never done that before. Her eyes glanced at the clock to find it was only 3:12.

"What's our song?"

"Honey, what –"

"Our song, Paul! What is it?"

"Goodnight Sweetheart."

Lois nodded, tears welling up in her eyes. Paul reached over and pulled her to him upon hearing her begin to sniff, relieved when she didn't stiffen. Her arms grasped desperately at him, her entire body curling into him as he held her.

"It was just a nightmare. I'm here."

It took a while for her to fall asleep. Paul gently began to stroke her hair once he heard her breathing slow, staring wide eyed in the dark. He'd never seen her have such an intense nightmare—and he couldn't stop thinking about how she'd flinched away from him. His grip on her tightened slightly as he closed his eyes, eventually managing to fall back asleep.

Lois woke peacefully at 4:30, glancing up from the tangle of limbs to see the clock confirm it. She gently extracted herself from Paul's arms. After getting her robe and slippers, Lois headed into the bathroom. An intense feeling of déjà vu filled her and she sighed, closing the door so she could turn on the light. She hung up her robe and pulled off her nightgown, about to get into the shower when she smelled her soap already on her skin. Blinking, she glanced down to see if it had spilled—and gasped. The bruise she'd gotten from falling down the stairs was on her leg.

"But…" Her hand shook as she reached down and touched it.

Lois winced at the pain.

It was real–and so was the dream.

Mary and Linda came downstairs that morning to find breakfast waiting for them on the table but their mother nowhere in sight. Mary, as hungry as ever, began to eat without a second thought. Linda, however, walked around until she found her mother curled up on a chair in the living room, scribbling furiously into a dark journal.

"Mom?" Linda asked, and Lois looked up sharply, managing not to jump.

"Oh, good morning, Linda."

Lois smiled, greatly relieved that Linda had called her 'mom.'

"What are you doing?"

"Oh, one of the other moms suggested we keep dream journals. I'm just writing mine down before I forget."

Linda slowly nodded.

"I'll come in and eat with you, dear."

Lois got up, closing the journal and putting it and her pen on the table. She walked over and took kissed the top of Linda's head, smiling as they walked back to the kitchen together.

"Morning, mommy!" Mary greeted them, Lois giving a nearly silent sigh of relief before replying, "Good morning, sweetheart."

She kissed Mary's cheek and sat down across from the girls.

"So, what's on the agenda for school today?" She asked, looking at Linda. Linda blinked in tired confusion, and Mary piped up.

"We're going to be doing division today! The teacher said she'd let me do the more advanced problems if I find them too easy."

"I'm glad. I had a little talk with her after she wouldn't let you do that last time." Lois turned back to Linda and she yawned.

"We finished our editing phase. Today we're writing new stories we can share." A strange expression crossed her mother's face, but only for a fraction of a second.

"Oh? What about?"

"I'm thinking of writing one about things disappearing and moving, but with something other than a person doing it."

This time the expression stayed—a cold, accusing look with unusually hard eyes. Linda squirmed slightly in her seat but felt like she couldn't look away from her mother's gaze.

"Could you remind me of what your last story was, dear?" Lois asked, her voice slightly stilted and almost interrogative. Linda blinked; her mother never seemed to forget anything, and the way she asked it almost made it seem like she already knew the answer. Out of the corner of her eye, she could see Mary hadn't noticed any of this.

"Yes, it was about an alien from another planet coming down to Earth and deciding to try and blend in to learn more about us. They thought it was easy because everyone in the neighborhood they landed in ran on a strict schedule."

The expression dissolved, very briefly replaced by relief before her mother smiled again. Her gaze warmed, and Linda was left even more confused.

"Oh yes. I remember."

Linda quickly finished her breakfast and ran upstairs to get changed and make her bed, leaving Mary alone with Lois.

"So, what was that art project you were doing the other week again?"

The child grinned through her eggs.

"The magazine and newspaper collage?" Mary asked, and Lois nodded.

"We finished it, remember, mommy? And I found a lady who looked like you in a pretty dress."

Lois tilted her head slightly to the side.

"Oh right. What colour was it again?"

"My *favourite* colour!"

"And what's that?"

Mary giggled.

"Don't be silly, you know it's purple."

Lois, relieved, gave a laugh and smiled conspiratorially at Mary, as if this had in fact been a joke.

"Of course I do, baby. Nothing gets past you!"

Lois smiled.

"Mommy's sure acting strange," Mary said jovially after she'd left the table, went upstairs, gotten dressed, and walked into Linda's room.

"Very," Linda agreed.

"Can you help me make my bed?"

Her sister nodded and followed her into the purple room. Linda glanced at the windowsill, staring for at the untouched pink powder. *Ants, huh?*

"C'mon!" Mary interrupted her, tugging at her hand, and Linda started to help Mary.

"What did she, uh, say to you, Mary?" Linda asked, a little surprised her more distracted sister had noticed Lois's antics.

"She asked me what my favourite colour is." Mary laughed, and Linda blinked.

"But she knows that."

"I know! She was being funny."

Linda forced a saccharine smile onto her face when Mary looked up to see if she agreed, and to her relief her sister took it as genuine.

"Yeah. Funny."

Linda avoided Lois as much as she could, relieved when Harold finally drove up and they were able to leave for school. Lois waved from the porch, hands shaking slightly. She had noticed how Linda had reacted, and as much as she wished she could explain why she'd interrogated her children, she couldn't tell them about the dream—if it even *was* a dream. Surely not, if the bruise was real. She had to be sure they were her real children.

But how could she be *sure?*

Lois shook the thought from her head as she picked up the newspaper and walked back inside the house, putting it on the table before walking up the stairs to wake up Paul. She paused just as she opened the door, a flash of what had happened before with the first version of her husband freezing her in place. She consciously forced herself to relax before she walked forwards, bending down in front of Paul and gently patting his shoulder.

"Dear," she murmured, too quietly to rouse him. She patted him again, but she knew her touch was too light. With a shaky breath, she shook him a little and he opened his eyes.

"Good morning, darling. How are you feeling?" he asked, blinking away the sleep in his eyes and sitting up.

"I'm alright."

He lifted a hand to run through his hair and she flinched, an expression of fear partially visible on the half of her face illuminated by the dim green of the clock's paint. Paul froze before forcing his hand back down.

Lois took a shaky breath, her hands withdrawing to her chest.

"I'm sorry," she whispered, "I just—it was the dream."

Paul turned on the light and gritted his teeth at how pale his wife looked. He slowly extended his hands and held them out, allowing her to pause before taking them.

"Maybe if you tell me about it, you'll feel better."

Her body visibly stiffened.

"I—I don't remember much of it. But there was someone who...someone who looked like you. Except...except—"

"Except he hit you?" Paul asked in a quiet voice, and she nodded.

"I know you would never do that." She got up and sat next to him on the bed, resting her head on his shoulder. He let go of one of her hands to put his arm around her.

"In the dream, that's how I knew it wasn't you. He just...he looked *just* like you, so I just...it's too fresh in my mind to not, to not react."

He turned and kissed her head. "I understand, Lois. I'll try not to move like that. I love you."

"I love you too."

After the alarm went off and Lois went downstairs to cook breakfast, Paul checked the untouched powder on the windowsill and jumped into the shower. Harold's idea of what was putting her so ill at ease was starting to feel more and more like the right explanation, especially if it was bad enough to cause a nightmare; Paul made a mental note to check in with Winston and see if he and Harold had worked together. He wouldn't feel any better until Lois felt better.

Paul came downstairs to find Lois had put breakfast on the table, the newspaper and a visibly hot cup of coffee at next to

111

his plate. She was sitting at her usual spot, a plate of food untouched in front of her. Lois hadn't seemed to notice him; she was scribbling something at rapid pace in a black journal.

"Everything looks great, honey," Paul said to bring her attention to him as he sat down, and she looked up and smiled.

"I try my best," she half joked, closing the journal and putting it down next to her seat with the pen atop it. There was silence as Paul began to eat. Lois moved her food around but ultimately ate little.

"Dear, you've barely touched your food," Paul finally said when he couldn't take the silence anymore.

"Hmm? Oh, I ate more than I usually did with the kids this morning, I'm sorry, dear."

"Are you alright? You're awfully quiet."

"Oh, yes, I was just thinking about tomorrow. We're having another knitting club meeting, and I was just…thinking, I suppose."

Paul got up and walked over to her, extending his hand. Confused, she took it and let him pull her up to stand. He put one hand on her shoulder and the other on her waist, giving an encouraging smile as she put her hands on his shoulders, catching on to the dancing position. Paul, in slow steps, began to lead them away from anything they could bump into, singing *A Kiss To Build A Dream On.*

After the first few lines, Lois leaned her head against Paul's chest and smiled, giggling a little when he imitated the trumpet between some of the verses. Once he got to the end of that song, the only pause between his next was a kiss on the top of her head. She hummed along when he started Frank Sinatra's *I Love You,* joining in about halfway through. Lois pulled her head up to meet his eye as they stopped dancing and finished the song, the grin on her face interrupted only when he leaned down to kiss her.

"I must be the luckiest woman on Earth." Lois said after Paul pulled away, slowly opening her eyes to find him smiling warmly down at her.

"Only if I'm the luckiest man." He replied, resting his

forehead against hers.

A minute of peace was interrupted when Lois suddenly said, "It's almost 8:10, you should get ready before you have to rush."

Paul glanced down at his watch to see it was 8:08 as she pulled away to get his lunch. He grabbed his keys from the bowl near the front door and was pulling his jacket on and walking into the garage as Lois came in with his lunch.

"Got your keys?"

He held them up, the blue 'P' visible.

Lois left a few lipstick marks on his cheek as she kissed him while he started the car.

"Oh, before you go, hold on a moment." She hurried into the front yard and disappeared, coming back a few moments with another blue Morning Glory blossom. Paul hoped this would be a new routine as she tucked it above his ear and wove the stem into some of his hair to keep it in place. Paul took the opportunity to kiss her again before she leaned out of the car.

"I love you."

"I love you too," Lois replied with a smile, and Paul was off.

Chapter 14

The minute he was gone Lois ran for the phone. She called Cynthia, who picked up after the first ring.

"Hello?"

"Cynthia, it's Lois."

"Did something happen?" She asked immediately, and Lois nodded before replying, "Yes, but I'll have to explain it."

"I have time."

Lois sighed in relief and sat down to recount what had happened.

"I'm glad you called. Nobody else has been having any nightmares like that, but make sure you write it down in a journal and –"

"I am."

"Good. And keep a close eye out for anything else that might happen. I know you'll know if something's in the wrong place."

Lois nodded.

"Alright. Yes. I will. Thank you."

Lois was about to say goodbye when Cynthia added, "And Lois?"

"Hmm?"

"It's alright. It'll be okay. You're not alone."

Lois bit her lower lip.

"I know. Thank you. Goodbye."

"Call me if anything else happens. Goodbye."

Lois scrutinised the whole house as she did her daily cleaning, but nothing was out of the ordinary. None of the thick lines of powder on the windowsills had been disturbed, none of the locks were open, and nothing wasn't as she'd left it.

Relieved, Lois rushed through her daily exercises and finished her diary entry. It was difficult to get through it at times, as she'd been absolutely scrupulous, but soon she was tucking it into a drawer of her vanity and hurrying out to do some gardening.

She was half buried by her tomato plants when her internal clock went off, alerting her that her children would soon be at the door. She got up and unlocked the back door, let herself in, and relocked it, hurrying upstairs to change out of her dirty gardening clothing.

Mary and Linda were knocking on the door by the time had changed and prepared their snack, waiting patiently as their mother unlocked the door and let them in.

"Hello, Linda, hello, Mary." She greeted, and Mary smiled while Linda kept a close eye.

"How was school today?"

"Good! I got to do a lot of problems that were meant for the older kids!" Mary informed her cheerfully.

They sat down at the table and Lois looked over at Linda as Mary continued, "We're going to be getting our collages back next week, too, mommy, so you can see it!"

"That's great, honey! I can't wait."

Lois looked from Linda's concerned face to Mary's excited one. Mary nodded in agreement and scarfed down several pieces of fried ham before quickly exiting to the living room to play music as she usually did.

"Mom," Linda finally said as Lois turned back to her.

"Yes, honey?"

"Why were you acting like that this morning?"

To Linda's surprise, Lois looked sad.

"Linda, I apologise. I know it must have felt like I was interrogating you. I didn't mean to do that, and it was wrong of me. I had a bad dream last night and because of it I was feeling a little off this morning," she explained, reaching her hands out over the table. Linda took them, relieved her mother wasn't angry.

Lois gave her a squeeze.

"I'm just a little nervous over all this talk about things going missing. If I start to act like that again, I don't mean it to be cruel—I just like to make sure everything is like it's supposed to be."

Linda blinked.

"So, you just want me to let you know it's me?" She asked, familiar enough with how real nightmares could seem. Lois nodded, relieved Linda understood.

"How about we have a code phrase? You ask me a question, and I give you an answer so you know it's me. But not a regular answer or phrase, so you know," Linda suggested, and Lois smiled.

"That's my girl. What should it be?"

After some discussion, Lois and Linda agreed upon the question and answer being, "How were you feeling in the dead of night?" "Like the jokers in a deck."

Paul, his store having been so busy that day that he was running low on nearly all his stock, finally got the chance to call Winston at 4 o'clock. The phone rang, and rang, and rang…he wasn't at his office. Disgruntled, Paul called his house.

"What happened?"

"Cynthia? Nothing, I just—is Winston there?" Paul asked.

"Oh!" Cynthia sounded flustered as she quickly replied, "I thought you were someone else. Hello, Paul. No, he's not here. I believe he's at the library with Harold."

Finally, some good news.

"Ah, thank you, Cynthia. Sorry if I interrupted anything."

"No, everything's fine. Goodbye, Paul."

There was something saccharine about that sentence, but Paul didn't have the time to dwell on that. He rung up the library, getting a librarian who asked him to hold the lane while they went and fetched Winston.

"Yeah, thanks. Hello? Paul?"

"Winston, I take it you've been doing some good work?"

"Just looking some things up, you know," he said hesitantly. Paul got the feeling the librarian was still there.

"Can I take this into another room? It's private," Paul heard Winston ask someone. He didn't catch the response, but Winston grunted. There were a few seconds of silence.

"Alright, they're gone. Just me, you, and Harry now."

There was another grunt, which Paul recognised as Harold.

"What have you found?"

"Sad to say, I think Harry may have a point," Winston admitted, and Paul swallowed whatever explosive reaction he was bound to have.

"Go on," he said instead.

"We've been looking into some old books in the library, old cases and records I have access to. There are some bouts of reports about unsolvable cases where things went missing, only for reports to later indicate that the person found the objects in their own homes. The books cover more than Rose Park, and I think that this might be something huge. I know it sounds ridiculous, and you know I hate this, but I have to consider that this might be something else. Something like Harold thinks."

Paul was silent for a moment as he considered this.

"Yeah?" His exasperated tone belied a cold sensation of fear in his heart; Paul desperately didn't want this to be something he had no control over, and thus couldn't protect his family from. However, there was almost no doubt now that it was something else.

"I confiscated a lot of records kept here. I don't want to cause a panic in case someone goes rooting around in here, especially since I saw some curious kids in the archives. I'm taking them back to Harold's. We're going to go over it further at the garage. Can you come over after dinner and work with us?"

Paul gritted his teeth. This was the first evening in two days he'd be able to spend time with his wife—he wanted to be with her.

"But I need to be with Lois."

"Paul, I don't like this situation, but maybe if we stay together, we can do *something*. She and the other wives are already whispering all about this on their own. I don't think she'll mind if you're not around for a few hours. Besides, if Patricia and Cynthia haven't told us anything, I doubt Lois will tell you anything."

"I *need* her to tell me, but…she doesn't think I'll believe her," Paul replied immediately, voice dripping with guilt.

"You can talk with her about it later. This is important."

Paul sighed.

"Alright. I'll see you after dinner."

Lois was calm and happily starting dinner when Mary came in to ask if she could play outside.

"The door's locked," Mary explained.

"Oh, yes, I'll come unlock it for you."

Lois glanced at the timer she'd set before grabbing her keys and walking with Mary to the back door on the other side of the house.

Once Mary was set up on the porch, Lois paused before saying, "When you want to come back in, Mary, just knock and I'll come over, alright? I want to keep this locked."

Mary nodded, so Lois closed the door and locked it again.

She hummed as she headed back over to the kitchen, stepping into the anteroom to put her keys in the bowl. It was after she dropped them in that she paused, her heart dropping in her chest. Lois closed her eyes for a second before looking at the keys again: a deep blue 'P' was hanging from the keyring.

Lois was at the phone and dialing for Cynthia immediately. Cynthia picked up after two rings, the sound of Jules saying something audible in the background.

"Yes?"

"Cynthia? It's Lois."

"What happened?" Cynthia asked immediately, and Jules stopped talking.

"I just put the keys back and they're Paul's. Mine have an 'L' and his have a 'P' hanging from the keyring, and this morning I *know* he drove off with his, but now they're here. They're here and I don't know how they got switched," Lois rattled off, her voice purposefully quiet in case Linda might have been able to hear her.

"What is it, mom?" She heard Jules ask, "You look worried—"

"Nothing that concerns you, Jules, just go out with your friends."

A pause.

"That's not even subtle…you can't explain that by someone breaking in. How would they manage to switch your keys with neither of you noticing? And I assume you haven't left the house?"

Lois shook her head vigorously as she said, "No."

"Alright. Don't forget to write that down and keep any eye out for anything else small like that. Okay?"

"Okay."

"Lois, I was thinking since this is the first time something's happened to you we could meet up tonight after dinner. Take the car and drive into town, go to the park or somewhere else quiet, and talk it out."

"That sounds like a good idea," Lois said, relieved.

"Excellent. I'll ask if anyone else can come with us."

Another voice was audible in the background of Cynthia's call, this one May's.

"I've got to go. Are you alright?"

"Yes."

"Okay. Goodbye."

"Goodbye."

Lois was wary as she finished the brunt of dinner, but she made sure not to let it get to her for the sake of her children. It was with a great sigh of relief that she finally heard Paul, late, pulling into the garage and pulling down the door. Even if she couldn't tell him about anything, his presence was still a comfort. She forced herself to stay at the stove to make sure the vegetables didn't burn, turning only when he walked into the kitchen.

"Hello, love," he greeted, kissing her cheek and wrapping his arms around her from behind. He might as well make the most out of the time he'd actually be with her that day.

"How was work?"

"Oh, lots of business today. We'll certainly be able to get Linda that camera for her birthday. Uh, Lois, I just wanted you to know that I'm going to be meeting Harold and Winston after dinner. We wanted to talk about something."

Lois nodded.

"I'm actually going to be meeting Cynthia after dinner. She wanted to show me new knitting pattern." A lie, but a believable one.

Paul moved to set the table as Lois took the pan off the burner and moved the vegetables onto a serving dish. She'd just managed to succeed in hiding her feelings towards the key situation when she looked up at Paul and froze.

Having been mostly paying attention to cooking, she hadn't gotten a good look at him until now; clearly visible as he set up the utensils was the Morning Glory blossom tucked behind his ear, except it was not blue.

It was red.

Paul did a double take as he glanced up from the finished setting, paying more attention just in time to notice all the colour draining from his wife's face.

"Lois? What is it?"

"That flower was blue when I gave it to you," she said before she could stop herself, realising too late that she shouldn't bring too much attention to the strange events. Paul paled as well, pulling the flower from his hair to look at it. It was, in fact, red; he knew for a fact Lois didn't grow any red flowers.

"Lois, I—" He started, furrowing his brows in confusion, but she interrupted, "I must have grabbed one from Nancy's yard by accident."

Paul blinked and looked back up at her, seeing her expression had smoothed over.

"Are you sure?"

"Yeah, honey, I was in a rush to give it to you, I'm sure I just picked the wrong one."

Paul knew it had been blue when she gave it to him, but he couldn't say anything so close to dinner—the kids would be concerned if it was late, and he didn't want to involve them in the local horrors at all if possible. He nodded as if he believed her.

"Here, I'll take your keys to get Mary off the back porch,

can you go upstairs to get Linda?" Lois asked before Paul could reconsider his position.

"Oh, yes, it's nearly 6 o'clock, isn't it? Sure, love, here you are," he pulled the keys out of his pants pocket and handed them over, kissing her cheek before heading upstairs. Once he was out of sight, Lois looked down at the keys.

There was a small clatter as they dropped to the ground, not loud enough for Paul or Linda to hear from up the stairs. Lois's hands were shaking as she stared wide eyed at the keys now on the linoleum; they had a deep blue 'P' on them. She hurried to the key bowl and saw that it was now her keys in them.

Lois forced herself to calm down as she went back into the kitchen, picked up Paul's keys, and went to the back porch to get Mary. She couldn't dwell on that right now; it was too close to dinner to call Cynthia and tell her about it, and at any rate, Paul and Linda would be down too quickly for her to tell the other housewife anything.

"Mary, it's dinnertime," Lois announced in a calm voice after she unlocked the back door.

"Okay, mommy!" She replied, gathering her homework and bouncing into the house.

Lois locked the back door and put the keys back in the bowl, not even looking at them as they dropped. She took a deep breath and walked into the kitchen to see Paul had brought Linda down, plastering a smile on her face as she sat down and they ate dinner.

Paul came up to Lois with her coat as she was getting ready to head over to Cynthia's.

"Oh, Paul, I made two blankets last meeting and forgot to give them to you," Lois said as she gestured to the guest room where she kept her knitting club bag. The almost constant feeling of unease in Paul's chest grew at this; in the past five days alone Lois had forgotten to do more things than she had in the past five years.

"I just wanted to remind you that you can tell me anything, Lois," he said as he took her hands. A flash of another expression crossed her face for just a second before she was smiling again.

"I know, darling. I've got to go, but I will tell you that I love you."

She kissed his cheek. As she was pulling back Paul held his hand to the side of her face and gently guided her back so he could kiss her properly.

"I love you too."

Paul watched from the porch until Lois was across the street, at Cynthia's door. She could feel his eyes on her, turning and giving a last wave before she knocked on the door and was let in.

"Lois! I'm just about ready to go, just wait right there." Cynthia immediately disappeared. It seemed May and Jules were elsewhere, the house almost entirely quiet. Winston appeared and surprised Lois.

"Oh! Hello, Lois."

He almost sounded nervous.

"Hello, Winston. Paul told me he was going to meet up with you and Harold tonight."

Winston nodded shortly.

"Yeah, I'm just about to head out now. I'll see him in a little bit." He explained as he pulled his shoes on. It would appear that they had given up on the lockbox, since there were shoes scattered all around the anteroom.

Winston paused in front of Lois, one hand on the doorknob. He put his other on her shoulder, turning to her with an unusually serious look.

"Paul really loves you, Lois. No matter what. More than anything."

Lois blinked at him, surprised. She was unable to muster a response by the time he nodded, opened the door, and left. She was still staring at the space where he'd been when she heard him start up the cruiser and leave the driveway, unblocking the garage door.

Chapter 15

"Finally, he's gone. Alright, come on, Lois." Cynthia reappeared, bringing Lois through the kitchen to the garage. Cynthia pulled the garage door up while Lois climbed into the passenger seat, pushing Winston's words out of her mind by the time the other wife had climbed in and started the car.

"Patricia and Nancy are the only others who are free, so we're going to stop at Patricia's first. Nancy's already there, Sean was apparently over her house for dinner." Lois nodded as they drove off, silent when they stopped and let the other two in.

The ride was quiet as they went into town, all of them bristling with the knowledge of what was happening but unwilling to start the conversation. After some wandering around, Cynthia eventually stopped at the park. At this time of night it was dead quiet, nobody around for at least a mile.

The four of them got out and walked in silence to the bandstand, lifting their skirts and settling down on the wooden platform.

"Cynthia told me about the dream, are you okay?" Patricia asked first, breaking the silence.

"About as fine as I can be."

Patricia took Lois's hands. Nancy, who had sat down next to her sister in law, put an arm around her.

"Did anything else happen?" Nancy asked seriously, and Lois nodded.

"Tell us all about it."

"Yes, alright. Yesterday, like I said, nothing happened, but that night I went to bed and had a dream. I think." Lois went on to describe the experience, her friends adopting expressions of horror despite already knowing the basic storyline from Cynthia.

"After I woke up, I thought it was just a horrid nightmare,

but then I discovered this."

She pulled her skirt up to show the deep bruise that went from mid-thigh to just below her knee, slightly above where her skirt ended. The others gasped; it was a nasty bruise.

"Then, today, a few small things happened. I—I don't really understand them. I called Cynthia about one, but there was a second one that happened just before dinner."

Lois explained the key situation, clearly worried that she'd imagined it all.

"It must have happened, right?"

They nodded, but Lois was not convinced.

"The other thing was also like that. Small. I took a blossom from the front yard and put it behind Paul's ear before he left, one of my morning glories. And what colour are my morning glories?"

"Blue," The three women immediately responded, fully aware of Lois's monochrome garden.

"Well, when he came home, the blossom in his hair was red. Red! But I know he didn't switch it out, because it was still tangled in his hair the way I'd done it for it to stay. It was my flower, but it was *red*. I, I don't know what's happening, but I feel like...I don't know what to think."

Nancy squeezed her arm as the others gave her sympathetic looks. The conversation shifted to the others telling about similar things happening to them; seeing things that changed later. Lois couldn't listen for very long, the sensation of not being able to trust her own eyes making her physically nauseous. After a short while, she abruptly excused herself to take a short walk.

Lois cleaned herself up as best she could in the park, opening her contact to check herself in the mirror. Lois was not a tan woman, but she looked incredibly pale. Her eyes had watered, so she quickly used her handkerchief to prevent any of her eyeliner or mascara from dripping down onto her cheeks. She sniffed, coughing and spitting at the grass. It was alright. She was alright.

She walked back to the bandstand to find her it empty. Nobody was there.

What?

Lois glanced around to see that there were a few stray couples roaming the park now, laughing as if there was nothing wrong. She walked over to the park entrance and Cynthia's car was gone.

They couldn't have all left, had they?

"Lois, are you alright?" Patricia asked. Lois turned to see her friend in a different dress, Harold by her side. Both of them were smiley aside from some mildly concerned looks.

What was happening?

"Oh, yes, just got a little nauseous from that conversation." Patricia blinked.

"What conversation?"

Lois's eyebrows furrowed.

"Uh."

Was she dreaming again? Was what was happening real?

"A conversation I was having with Nancy. You know how she can get." Lois recovered quickly, and Patricia gave her a sympathetic look.

"Where is she, anyway?"

Lois blinked and looked around with wide eyes.

"Oh, I thought they were right behind me! Silly me. Nancy, Paul, and James must still be further in the park. I'm going to go catch up with them." Lois just barely managed to keep panic out of her voice, laughing slightly unnaturally.

"Well, alright. Good evening, Lois. Tell Nancy and them I say hello," Patricia said, Harold mirroring her statement. Lois quickly nodded and walked off, starting to run when she got a bit of a distance away. Her throat choked up and she kept going, the park melting away from her consciousness as she sank into her thoughts. Had none of it been real? Had she imagined the past few days?

"Lois!"

She was full tilt sprinting by the time she got back to the bandstand and heard her name, stopping short when she saw—

Patricia, Nancy, and Cynthia were all staring at her.

Lois looked around wildly—the park was deserted yet

again. Nobody for at least a mile. Dead quiet. They were alone.

"Lois, what's the matter?"

"How did you come from that direction? You went the other way."

"Why are you running?"

Their questions were slowly processed as she walked back up to them, sitting down heavily next to Nancy. Her breathing was quick and she was shaking.

"I, I. I—I, you, you remember?" She stammered, and several pairs of eyebrows knitted as Nancy put a hand on Lois's shoulder and had her turn to face her.

"Lois. What happened?" she asked, voice concerned but firm.

"I, I went and I, when I came back from my walk, you were all...you were all gone. I went back to the street and the car was gone. There were people walking around the park, and, and Patricia and Harold came up to me. They asked me what was wrong, as if—as if none of this had even happened. Like none of it was real."

Nancy pulled her sister into a hug, the others blinking and exchanging expressions of fear.

"How...how could that have happened? We were all right here, talking the whole time," Patricia stuttered out.

"Lois, how long do you think that was happening?" Cynthia asked gently, and Lois looked up from Nancy's shoulder.

"At, at least twenty minutes," Lois managed to say.

"You got back from your walk ten minutes ago, at the maximum," Cynthia said, and Nancy squeezed her sister a little tighter when Lois's body seized.

They decided to leave not long after Lois got back, everyone just wanting to get back and see their children. The car ride was dead silent aside from Cynthia telling everyone to call her if anything else happened as she dropped them off—Patricia first, and then Nancy and Lois together.

"Are you sure you'll be alright? I know you want to tell him," Nancy asked as they watched Cynthia pull into her garage.

"He won't believe me," Lois replied, her voice small and sad. Nancy closed her eyes for a moment before putting her hands on Lois's shoulders.

"Lois, you haven't known Paul as long as I have, but let me tell you. That boy loves you more than anything, and he trusts you. If you tell him about this, I think he'll believe you. I know what Cynthia said, but with all this happening…I know you tell him everything. You should tell him this."

Lois blinked, staring at Nancy before slowly nodding.

"I'll. I'll think about it," Lois promised, Cynthia's warning still fresh in her mind. Nancy bit her lip before nodding.

"Alright. Goodnight, Lois."

"Goodnight, Nancy."

Nancy watched as Lois climbed up the stairs and let herself into the house, giving a little wave before disappearing inside. Nancy only left to go to her house next door when she heard the lock click.

Paul still wasn't back yet when she arrived, so she headed into the living room and sat down on a sofa chair to sort through her thoughts.

Chapter 16

Not long after Lois left for Cynthia's, Paul had told Linda to make sure Mary got to bed at eight and left for Harold's garage. Winston's cruiser was already in the parking lot when he'd arrived, so it was not a surprise when Winston opened the door to the garage.

"I heard your car. Come on in."

Winston led Paul through Harold's office and up a spiral staircase to the loft. Harold was sitting at a desk littered with papers and old books, a chair pulled up next to him that Winston had obviously been using. Harold nodded at him.

"Pull up a chair."

Paul grabbed a folding chair from where it was leaning against the wall and brought it over to the desk, he and Winston sitting down together. Harold tapped a document on the top with his finger.

"It's going to get worse if we don't do something soon. We're dealing with something incredibly powerful. We've been reading old police records and there have been cases like ours in the past, where people reported objects of theirs going missing or moving only to find them later. Winston looked into some of the residents cited in the cases, and it seems like they all moved, so we can't really ask them, but a few of them stayed for long enough that things got worse than they are right now. They reported it as being caused by gas leaks because of what they saw."

Paul glanced down at the document, eyes widening.

"Terrible dreams that were actually reality. Time seeming to go back and restart. People disappearing and reappearing elsewhere. As far as I know, that hasn't happened to anyone yet. But if it does, it can only get worse from there. Whatever's doing this, it's going to make it so we can't trust anything—not the people around us, not our eyes, not our ears. Nothing. Not even our minds. And who knows what happens next?"

Paul felt nauseous.

"And she's going through it alone," He breathed. Harold reached behind Winston and put a hand on his shoulder.

"Paul, ask her if anything's happened to her tonight. Tell her you know it's supernatural. Tell her you'll believe her, and she'll explain everything. She must want to tell you," Harold suggested.

Pale, Paul nodded.

"Now, before you run off, we have to talk about our game plan. The people living in this area before it was Rose Park left because they thought it was full of criminals and leaking gas, but if possible, I'd like everyone to be able to stay here," Winston said.

"What are we supposed to do against something like this?" Paul asked.

"I don't know. But we have to figure something out. Me and Harold took out a lot of old lore books. Maybe we can find something in here about what it could be."

Paul, Harold, and Winston read book after book for several hours, but they didn't find anything helpful. Most of it was just legend—which Winston readily pointed out was false, much to Harold's chagrin—but the seeds of truth did not align with their situation. They were tired and defeated when they decided to turn in, driving back home in separate silence.

Paul walked in to find Lois sitting still on the couch, alone and contemplative. Checking his watch, he saw that it was a little after 10 o'clock at night. He'd been with Winston and Harold for nearly three hours.

"Hello, love. Why are you still up?"

She shook her head and turned to look at him. He walked over and sat next to her, blinking as she wrapped her arms around him and nestling into his chest. Paul put his arms around her, pulling back to lie down as he tangled their legs together.

"I was just thinking," Lois explained, her voice slightly muffled by his shirt. Paul kissed the top of her head, sighing silently. He could only imagine what she and Cynthia had gotten up to talking about. Paul's fingers slipped into Lois's hair as he cradled her head, his other arm making sure she stayed close to him.

"Lois?"

"Hmm?"

"Has anything strange happened to you in the past few days?"

His wife's entire body tensed up. Paul's eyes closed tightly, biting his lip. Something had happened, and she hadn't told him. Of course something had. Harold was right, as usual.

"Lois, please," he pleaded, his voice soft, and her grip on him tightened.

"Nothing really," she assured him quietly.

"If it bothers you, it's something."

"I just…I thought I used your keys while you were at work, but you came home with them, so I must have been mistaken. And the flower, you know. I thought it was blue. It's really nothing."

Paul waited, but she didn't say anything more.

"Are you sure that's all, dear?"

"Yes," she replied immediately. A little *too* immediately.

Paul sat up and brought Lois with him, his hand gently resting at her chin so she'd look at him.

"Lois, are you sure that's all?"

She sucked in her lower lip.

"Please tell me."

"It's—I fell asleep while I was out with Cynthia and had another nightmare, that's all."

Paul found this quite unusual, considering that his wife's strict adherence to her timetable more than carried into her sleep schedule; seeds of doubt at how much of a dream it was were difficult to ignore. *Terrible dreams that were actually reality.* All those worse things they thought were yet to come were happening to his wife, right now.

He had to remain calm.

"I think I'll go to bed a little early tonight."

Lois started moving to get up when Paul scooped her up into his arms.

"I'll join you." Paul kissed her forehead as she wrapped her arms around his neck and blinked in surprise. He carried her up the stairs and into the bedroom, letting her land gracefully on her feet next to her closet. Paul kissed her gently before going to his drawers and changing into pyjamas, getting into bed just as Lois went into the bathroom and began to wash off her makeup. He could see she was still worried, and he intended to get her to tell him the full story once they were both lying down.

Lois walked out of the bathroom and stretched at the end of the bed. Paul was about to turn out the light when he let out a gasp and quickly crossed over to the other side of the bed, where Lois was staring at him in confusion.

"What? What is it?"

"Your leg!" he cried out, and Lois looked down at her bruise. After wearing a skirt that had hidden it all day, she forgot that her nightgowns were not long enough to do the job.

Paul pulled her onto the bed and slowly lifted her nightgown skirt up until he came to the top of the bruise, a few inches below her hips. His hand was shaking slightly as he gently touched the edge of it, looking up at Lois as she winced.

"What happened?" he demanded, clearly concerned.

"I fell down the stairs this morning."

"What? I would have heard that. When this morning?"

"Well, well after you *left*, dear," Lois quickly explained, but it was obvious that she was lying.

"Lois."

She nervously licked her lips.

"I don't know."

"What?"

"I don't know when it happened."

Her voice was quiet, so he went silent to give her a chance to explain.

"I. That dream I told you about? I fell down the stairs in it,

131

and I saw that I was going to bruise in the dream…I woke up with this." Before he could say anything, she held her hands up to her face.

"That sounds ridiculous," she said cynically, clearly chiding herself.

"Lois, a lot of strange things are happening. Strange, *supernatural* things. That doesn't sound ridiculous," he assured her, gently pulling her hands from her face.

"I understand."

His expression, so full of love and concern, was the last straw for Lois. She broke down and told him everything; the other wives' stories, the full details of the dream, the keys, the flower, the second dream, absolutely everything. By the end of it she was shaking and speaking at a rapid pace, licking her lips and wringing her hands.

Paul made sure she was looking at him before he said, "I believe you."

Lois stopped moving, staring at him with a mix of awe and deep gratitude.

"I don't know what's causing this, but we'll get through it. Together."

Lois quickly nodded and Paul pulled her into a hug, slowly transitioning into a lying position. They fell asleep together, the lights still on, at the end of the bed.

Something woke Lois at 2:00; a nagging feeling deep in her chest. She sat up to find it was dark and she was under the covers. Paul was asleep on his side of the bed without so much as a leg in contact with her. The feeling within her grew; they had fallen asleep with the light on. Paul had been asleep when she drifted off; when would he have moved her, turned off the light, and rolled away?

Blinking, Lois got out of bed and went into her vanity, pulling out her journal. Carrying it into the bathroom and turning on the light, Lois set herself up on the edge of the tub. She reread the dream before adding the other events to it, up until the nightmare at the club meeting.

Lois glanced at the door, thinking of how she'd woken up; this had been happening enough that she knew better than to ignore it. Something had changed. At some point after she'd fallen asleep, everything had been changed again—she couldn't trust her memories. Lois got up and turned off the light, putting the journal away before crawling into bed next to Paul.

She gently shook him and he blinked awake.

"Hmmm? Lois, it's…its 2 in the morning, are you alright?" He mumbled, clearly still half asleep.

"Dear, do you remember what we talked about last night?" She asked quietly.

"Something about there being another meeting tomorrow night."

"Okay. Thanks, dear."

"You're welcome," he murmured, yawning before turning over and wrapping her up loosely in his arms. Within seconds he was asleep again.

Lois stared up at the ceiling with wide eyes, consciously slowing her breathing. He didn't know. The great burden that had been lifted from her chest upon telling him returned twice over, along with the sickening knowledge that telling Paul was futile. Telling *anyone* was futile; if history could just be rewritten like that, if she couldn't trust her own eyes or ears…she was alone.

Lois didn't sleep for the remainder of the night.

At 4:00 she finally extricated herself from Paul's grip, making sure not to wake him. She couldn't take lying there anymore, the feeling of dread building up in her chest. Lois showered, got dressed, did her makeup, and was downstairs by 4:30. Once she reached the foot of the stairs she stopped short, eyes wide, heart pounding in her chest.

The small first floor showed the moonlight filtering through the French windows, bright and clear as it overlooked the city. Cars were driving below despite the late hour; the sound was so familiar that for a brief, foolish second, Lois thought nothing was wrong. Her and Paul's coats were hanging up next to the apartment door, near a small open kitchen and the main living space. The carpet felt worn under her feet as she stepped off the stairs, wandering around in awe. It had been years, but it felt like no time had passed.

Lois stood in the middle of her and Paul's old apartment. It had been many years since they had lived here, as they had moved to Rose Park not long after Linda was born.

Lois didn't know what to think as she wandered moon—eyed through the building. Everything was as it had been ten years ago; the lack of baby supplies made it clear that here, Linda didn't exist yet. Lois's breathing was rough and fast as she tried to make sense of what she was seeing. This could not be possible. What she was seeing couldn't be real.

Lois reached out and touched everything, feeling the countertops, the drapes, the coats; her old perfume was wafting from her jacket, both of which she had switched out years back.

It felt like several hours passed as she walked slack jawed around her old apartment. She was in the middle of a repeating thought process of how she could possibly be ten years in the past when the door rang. She walked over to it in a daze, opening it to find Winston.

What?

Lois blinked and looked past him, seeing her current yard. With a panicked look back into her house, she saw it was as it was supposed to be; the bottom floor of her home in Rose Park. Her breathing quickened and shaking hands rose to her face, running through her hair.

"Lois?" Winston asked, stepping inside and putting his hands on her shoulders.

"W—Winston, I, I'm sorry," she stuttered in a frightened murmur, not sure what to believe.

"Lois, I came over because Cynthia doesn't seem to remember anything. Right after knitting club we were talking about all the strangeness going on all over Rose Park, but at 2:00 I woke up knowing something was wrong. I asked her if anything had happened and she had no idea what I was talking about. I came over here to see if Paul remembered. Is he awake?"

Lois shook her head, reaching out and stopping Winston before he could head upstairs.

"He doesn't remember," she whispered, and Winston stared at her.

"I woke up at 2:00 with the same feeling. Last night I told him everything, but when I woke up I knew something was different. I asked him if he remembered what we spoke about last night and he didn't. He doesn't know. It's all been changed again..."

Lois started to panic.

Winston led her into the living room to sit down. He sat across from her, hands folding and refolding.

"What happened?" he asked, and Lois told him about everything that had happened to her—all the way up until when he'd knocked on the door. Winston listened with a steely expression, nodding solemnly.

"It's more noticeable than I thought," he said, and Lois nodded.

"Lois, who else have you told about all this?"

"Only the knitting club girls and Paul. And I wrote it down in a journal. That's all."

"Alright. I don't want too many people to be aware of this. There'd be a panic, and then it'd be harder to keep everything under control."

"I won't tell anyone else."

Lois gave a shaky sigh and buried her face in her hands.

"Winston, I just—I, I, with Paul not knowing, I don't have anyone. I don't know what to believe. Nothing I see is guaranteed anymore. I have to ask questions about everything, or, or I might get tricked again. Like how Paul and my girls were acting strangely, so I knew it was wrong. My *girls*...and, and whenever someone acts out of the normal, I have to—"

Lois stopped.

Winston, while friendly, was not the kind to come running to a friend's house at 2 in the morning. He rarely shared case information, even with his wife. If anything, he would have gone to the station—Lois knew from experience that Winston would head out very early if he got a hunch on a case or felt like something was wrong.

"I have to question everything," Lois said, looking up.

135

Winston was gone.

Chapter 17

Lois ran upstairs and ripped her journal out of the vanity drawer, flipping through its pages.

All of them were blank.

Paul woke up when his alarm blared to find his children gone and his wife sitting on the porch staring at nothing. Breakfast had clearly been made, as he could smell it, but when he glanced into the kitchen he saw his portion was still uncooked. Mary and Linda must have been over someone's house, as it was a Saturday.

Paul unlocked the front door and walked out onto the porch, sitting down in the chair closest to Lois's. She stared out toward the front garden, clearly unaware that he was there. The newspaper was still on the path and he got the impression that she'd sat down and lost track of time after the kids left.

"Lois?"

No response.

"Lois," he started a bit more forcefully, and Lois turned to him. Paul opened his mouth to say something—and froze.

Lois blinked.

"Paul?"

This time she was the one to get no response. Lois waved her hand in front of his face, but he didn't react. She poked him. Nothing. His expression didn't change, and she realised he wasn't breathing. Putting a hand to his chest, it became apparent his heart wasn't beating either. Lois should have felt terrified, worried her husband was dead, but he wasn't; she could see he wasn't, feel it in her bones. He wasn't dead, just...frozen.

Lois got up and stumbled down the porch steps, the silence of everything suddenly striking her. The wind had stopped blowing, the birds and bugs were silent—*everything* was still and silent. Lois dropped to her knees in the grass, staring at the Earth as it refused to turn.

She screamed.

Lois screamed into the void, as loud as she could, until she lost all her breath. She let it build back up and screamed again until her voice was sore and she couldn't anymore. She laid down on her side in the grass and sobbed, fists hitting the ground as she finally let herself stop bottling up her fear and react.

Her rough voice begged—*demanded*—the world give her an answer, an explanation, but there was none. She was alone and ignorant in the middle of a frozen wasteland, of which was rapidly feeling plasticine and false.

After an indeterminable amount of time, Lois sobered and stood back up. She walked back into the house, fixed her makeup, and left again, not bothering to lock the door. Now feeling rather like she was in the front row of a movie theatre and simply watching everything that was happening—or not happening, more accurately—she walked over to Nancy's house.

Looking through the window, she could see her in-laws and her two children at their kitchen table, caught in the middle of a frozen conversation. The next house showed a similar scene, and the next, and the next.

Lois, numb to everything at this point, walked all the way to town. Cars were stopped in the middle of the street, early risers standing mid-stride on the sidewalks. Lois walked past her husband's general store, the library, the bank—something was drawing her to the police station.

The lone observer approached the white steps, walking up and finding the door unlocked. She walked past a still secretary in the picture of conversation with one of the younger policemen, through the employee entrance, and into the offices. The officers there were all in the middle of working, eating, talking, writing; it was like she was walking through a museum.

Lois was beckoned onward until she got to Winston's

office. Without so much as a pause she pushed through the doors and walked in.

Winston was behind his desk, as statuesque as the others. She walked up to him, looking at the papers on his desk. They were all blank. Lois looked back up at Winston, seeing the consternation on his expression; it didn't take a genius to realise that these papers had not always been blank. She glanced around the office, wondering dimly why she had walked there when the papers on his desk caught her eye.

The page directly in front of Winston was not blank now.

Lois stared at the page, the word scribbled on it clearly readable but written in a scratchy, scrawling font. She pondered why it seemed like no human hand could have written it when Winston suddenly moved next to her; she stumbled back, falling over as he looked at her in shock.

"Lois? How did you get in here? Without me even noticing?"

She stared up at him in fear. He quickly got out of his chair and held a hand out for her. Shaking, she took it.

Hopefully this was really him.

"I, I walked here."

Winston blinked.

"You. You just appeared here. I was looking at my newly blank papers and—" He'd gestured to the desk and glanced at them as he spoke, freezing when he saw that one of them had writing on it.

"That one's not blank," he said, looking at Lois. She held up her hands to indicate she hadn't done it and he looked back at it.

"'Soon.'" He stared down at it in silence.

Slowly Winston looked up at Lois.

"Lois, how did you get in here?" He asked again, his voice slow and patient and vaguely frightened. Lois was reluctant to respond after what had happened that morning, but she needed to tell someone.

"Winston, did you visit me this morning?"

He shook his head.

Lois swallowed hard and nodded. "Maybe you should sit

down."

He sank into his chair, eyes following her as she walked to the other side of his desk and sat on one of the two chairs in front of him.

Lois told her entire story to him again, this time in an detached voice.

"Then Paul came outside, and he was about to say something when he froze. The entire world did. I walked here and nothing was moving. I, I don't know why I came *here*, exactly, but you were still as well. Every, everything was. *Everything* was. I came in and you were sitting here, staring at blank papers, and I was wondering how I'd even gotten here when I saw that one of the pages wasn't blank anymore, and then you woke up."

Winston had listened to the whole thing with an expression somewhere between validation and fear. He knew now that he was right, that Harold was right—that something bigger was at play here.

A snap decision was made, and he was about to say something when the phone rang. Lois jumped and Winston quickly reached for it.

"Police Chief's off—alright, alright. Hold on. Paul? Is that you?"

Lois's eyes went wide as Winston matched her gaze.

"What? Lois is missing? She—she *what?* She just disappeared? Yes. I know, I know she—I know! Slow down, will you, she's fine! Yes, I know, because she's here. Yes! Meet us at Harry's garage and I'll explain. And calm down before you start driving, I don't want you to crash. Yes. Goodbye."

"Come on," Winston said once the phone was down on the receiver, holding his hand out as he walked around the desk. Lois took it and they hurried out of the station, ignoring exclaimed questions about where he was going and how Lois had gotten in there. Winston quickly led her to his cruiser and they climbed in, his hands shaking slightly as he got the car in gear and drove off.

"What did Paul say?"

"He said you just disappeared. That one second you were there, and then you were gone. He was scared as hell. Still is, likely. It's a killer that he doesn't remember anything you told him, but we'll explain it to him, don't worry. He'll believe you."

Lois sighed shakily and nodded, wringing her hands as Winston sped to Harold's garage. Was there a point to telling him again?

Lois decided not to ask.

Winston parked in one of the few spots outside and hurried out, holding the door open for Lois just as Harold came through his door.

"You're keen. Something big just happened, but I don't know what," Harold said in greeting.

"Lois knows what happened. She can explain it."

"Oh? Are you alright, Lois?" Harold asked, turning to Lois with curiosity and putting a hand on her shoulder. She was visibly pale and shaking, but she nodded.

"Well—woah!"

Harold stepped to the side as Paul drove into the other free parking spot, the car screeching to a halt just short of crashing into the garage itself. He leapt out of the car and ran over, pulling Lois into a tight embrace.

"Alright, alright, she's fine, just like I told you."

Harold raised an eyebrow as Paul gently rocked Lois side to side, his grip on her visibly tight.

"I know you told me, but she was just *gone*, Winston." Paul responded in a hoarse voice.

"Is anyone else coming?" Harold asked, instead of the question he wanted to ask.

"No."

"Alright, come on, let's go in." He led them up to the loft. Paul—who had kept an arm around Lois the entire time—sat down on the couch with her, Winston taking the stool he'd used the night before as Harold leaning against his desk.

"Okay. Before the questions start flying, Lois is in the unique position of knowing most of the situation. Lois?" Winston stated, and all eyes turned to her. Paul's free hand took hers and she swallowed hard.

"Alright. I—before I say this, I just want to say, I, I don't understand any of it, and I know it's going to be hard to believe, but it's all true."

"We know," Harold said. Paul and Winston nodded.

"Okay. Here goes."

Lois told the whole story again, starting from the knitting club meeting all the way to Winston waking up from the time freeze. No detail was left out—every wife's story, small abnormality, Eldritch revelation, and the play by play of each strange event were all explained.

Paul seized up at the mentions of the other versions of him and of him having forgotten everything she'd told him. When she finished telling it, there was a heavy silence; Paul pulled Lois back into a hug and peppered kisses to the top of her head.

"I'll be damned," Harold said, shaking his head, "I knew something happened but...*damn*. Everything just stopped?"

Lois nodded.

"Then I was right. We're dealing with something incredibly powerful."

"Eldritch," Harold muttered, "I should have known. Makes full sense. Except they're beyond our control, beyond our world. There's nothing we can do. But..."

"But what?" Paul asked.

Harold shrugged but Winston started, "I think I have enough of an idea on that to help us. Lois, we were reading old police records and there have been cases like ours in the past, where people reported objects of theirs going missing or moving only to find them later. I looked into some of the residents cited in the cases, and they all moved, but—"

"It's here."

"What?" Winston asked after Harold interrupted him.

"The cases are all centralised here. You said after I told you about the socks that all the calls are only in Rose Park, not anywhere else. This never happened to me or anyone else I know before we moved here. If it's in past cases, maybe it only happens every so often, building up and then sinking away. Before this was a Levittown clone it housed very few people, and the town was miniscule—there weren't enough people to really make a deal of it, and like you said, they all left, thinking that it was a robber or whatever other things people think this is. It's here that's the problem, and now there's dozens and dozens of people stuck here suffering through whatever this is. Whatever is causing it, Eldritch or not, it's rooted in Rose Park."

Everyone was silent as Harold's statements sunk in. Lois leaned her head against her husband's shoulder, half to get a little closer and half to stop him from nervously kissing her.

"What are we supposed to do? Nobody is going to believe this. We don't even know what it is." Paul's voice was quiet and nervous.

"No, it's definitely not the way to go to try and convince everyone to move out. But we have to do *something*," Winston replied.

More silence.

"It'd take too long to make another town seem better."

"Rose Park isn't even halfway full, maybe if we made the town seem even more inhospitable, people would leave."

"That would take a long time, too, and this is clearly getting worse as time goes on."

The three men shot ideas out at each other as Lois sat silent, listening and thinking. Even with all this happening, part of her didn't want to leave; they'd settled in there with their children, established themselves with the general store, and lived there for eight years now. Even knowing that this would likely only get worse and that it would stop if she left Rose Park, an irrational part of her wanted to stay because this was her home now. Under normal circumstances, she'd only leave if she had to, like if something drastic happened. A freak accident, or—

"A fire."

"What?" The other three asked in unison.

"Everyone is settled here. The only way they'll leave is if they have to."

"Arson is a crime." Winston's immediate reply was one of

instinct rather than as a statement of his approval or disapproval.

"She's right," Harold said, and Winston blinked.

"I know," He sighed, putting his head in his hands and groaning, "We'll have to burn the whole town and neighborhood down."

"Not right now?" Paul asked immediately, Lois sitting up straighter.

"No, we can't do it right now. This will take some planning, and I want to move Cyn and the kids out of the town before we even begin to lay the groundwork," Winston assured him.

"I'll send Patricia and the kids to visit her mother. She's been meaning to, anyway."

"And I can send Cyn and the kids to her parents'. They've been complaining about not seeing us."

Paul looked to his wife, squeezing her hand.

"You and the kids could go to see my parents," he suggested.

"Honey, I don't think that's the best idea."

"What do you mean?" Paul asked, voice slightly rough.

"Paul, I'm the only one of the four of us who saw the whole world freeze. If something else happens and you forget, I might remember and be able to take care of the job. We have to stay together."

Paul opened his mouth to argue, but he couldn't think of any good retorts.

"But I want you to be safe."

"She'll be safer after the town is gone," Harold replied.

Paul sighed and nodded.

"Alright. Only the kids will go to mom and dad's. We'll stay here together."

After a few hours of discussion, it was decided that they would get their families and possessions out before Winston would call an evacuation. This would be excused as, ironically enough, a massive gas leak—which he explained was vague enough, dangerous enough, and difficult enough to disprove that everyone should be out of town quickly. Then, they would burn it down.

"Now, Lois, there's a knitting club meeting tonight, right?" Winston asked, and Lois nodded.

"Alright. Tell the girls about what happened and tell them you think it's getting worse and that they should consider leaving town for a while. Maybe say that you drove out of town and everything went away, and that the strangeness only returned when you did. Make them think that it's Rose Park and not just a general bending of space and time."

"Alright. I'll try."

Winston nodded.

"Okay. I've got to get back to the station before the boys get even more confused. Everybody keep in touch over the phone and call anytime anything happens. Especially you, Lois. Let me know if *anything* happens, no matter how small."

Lois nodded.

"We should be getting back home, too," Paul said, clearly not intending on opening the store that day.

Harold waved them off after they got into their cars and drove, Winston turning to head for the station and Paul taking Lois back in the direction of their house.

"Thank the stars you're alright," Paul said once they were out of sight of the garage, as if he was worried Harold would have been able to hear them.

"You were just *gone*, Lois. And when I came out to talk with you in the first place, you were so distracted. I had no idea all of this was happening to you, and with you having told me, and then me forgetting…I'm so sorry."

"It's not your fault, Paul," Lois reassured immediately.

"I know. But I still should have been there for you."

Once they got home and locked the car up, Paul called his parents and planned for them to pick Linda and Mary up on Sunday afternoon. Once that was settled, they headed up to their bedroom. Lois showed him the journal, which was as empty as it had been when she'd checked it that morning. Paul ran a hand through his hair before beckoning her to the bed, wrapping his arms around her and lying down.

"I am here for you, always. If I forget again, tell me everything, because I will believe you. Okay? I'll always believe you," he promised.

Lois nodded into his chest.

"I love you."

"I love you, too."

Chapter 18

Lois and Paul laid there for several hours, their eyes closed but neither of them able to sleep. They only moved when Lois sat up, her internal clock alerting her that the kids would be home from Nancy's for lunch soon.

"What is it?"

"I need to get lunch ready for the girls."

"Oh, I'll help."

They both got up and walked downstairs, distracting themselves with making sandwiches, cutting apples into slices, and coating the slices with peanut butter. Paul was amazed by Lois's instinct to leave the house at just the right time to see Linda and Mary leaving Nancy's house next door.

"Hi, daddy! What are you doing home?" Mary asked as Lois took her and Linda's hands, Paul taking Mary's other hand.

"I thought I'd come home early to surprise you."

Lois glanced at Linda, who clearly had other interpretations of why Paul was there but kept them to herself.

"Kids, tomorrow your grandparents are coming to pick you up and take you for the weekend," Paul announced, and Lois nodded. Mary grinned, but Linda was curious.

"Oh? Why?"

"Well, they want to see you."

Linda looked over at Lois. The expression Lois gave her must have answered her question, because Linda nodded.

"Okay. That sounds fun."

Dinner that night was normal, the only real questions of note being from Linda about their grandparents.

"Grandma Heather and Grandpa James, not Grandma Serena and Grandpa Micky. Your cousins might even join you, but we're not sure yet," Paul explained.

"It's just for a few days. Me and your mother are staying here."

"What about school?"

"We'll make sure your teachers understand."

Mary looked at Linda conspiratorially, and Linda gave her sister a patient smile before nodding.

"Okay."

"You know our phone number," Lois said, and Linda nodded.

Paul stayed right next to Lois until it was time for her to leave for the knitting club meeting.

"I'll call James and tell him I'm sending the kids with mom and dad and that he might want to do the same," he promised at the door, giving Lois one last kiss.

"I'll do what Winston said and try to get the others out of here."

Paul nodded, and she gave a small smile.

"I'll be close by. Don't worry," she reminded him, and she gave his hand a squeeze before leaving. Paul watched her disappear down the street in the direction of Eleanor's house, wishing he could stay with her.

That meeting everyone had a nightmare to share; it was obvious things were getting worse. Patricia had seen two Daniels that morning and it took her half an hour to find Sean, while Eleanor reported that Brian had completely disappeared only to reappear at least three times. They all paled in comparison to what Lois reported, however; everyone was silent as she recounted the world stopping. She then changed the ending—instead of ending up at Winston's, she said that she'd left town and time had resumed.

"It felt like a huge weight was lifted. When I walked back into town everything was moving again, but that heavy feeling was back. I think it's Rose Park, not us."

"That's all I need to hear. I'm getting out of here," Nancy said, shaking her head.

"That's not a bad idea. Winston already wants me and the kids to visit my parents," Cynthia said.

"Yes. Harold says I should take mine to see my mother.

He's got the right idea. He knows something is going on and he wants us out."

Lois turned to Nancy.

"Heather and James are coming down tomorrow to take Linda and Mary for a few days. I'm sure they'll be happy if you, James, Maureen, and Jane join them."

Nancy nodded.

"Yeah. Yeah, I think I'll call them. What about you and Paul?"

"We've got some things to do here before we do anything."

Nancy furrowed her brows.

"I don't want you to stay here more than you have to."

"I won't. We won't be here for much longer."

By 8:30 the group consensus was that everyone would make plans to move out. All the plans were insistent but tentative, and Lois was privately relieved that Winston's gas leak plan would speed everything up. They adjourned a little after nine, Lois happy to have convinced all of her friends to leave.

"How'd it go?" Paul asked the second Lois stepped through the door, having heard her keys in the lock.

"They all want to leave, and Nancy said she'd call your parents."

"I called James, and he already did. He said he was going to take Nancy and go up with them. He wants to clear his head before looking back over the case. Thankfully, by the time his head is clear it shouldn't be a problem anymore."

Lois smiled.

"I also checked through our papers. The store's ensured, and if it's destroyed in an accident we'll be refunded. Same for the house. After this happens we'll have plenty of money to set up somewhere else."

Lois grinned and wrapped her arms around her husband.

"Soon, everything will be back to normal."

Lois and Paul slept well that night, with Lois waking up at 5:00 like she always used to. The kids slept in as she started the beginnings of breakfast, leaving it uncooked as she went outside. Lois took the newspaper in and walked into her bedroom, about to shake her husband awake when she paused.

He was just going to insist on staying with her, so there wasn't much of a point to waking him up earlier than he had to rise. Lois turned his alarm off and woke up Mary and Linda, suggesting that they go over to Nancy's.

Paul woke up at 10:23, a bit confused as to why he felt like he'd gotten so much sleep.

"Lois?" He asked pointlessly, blinking and glancing at the clock to gather the time. He got up, got dressed, and left the room to find the attic hatch open and the ladder down. Paul was about to climb up to see what Lois was doing up there when she came down with a box balanced precariously against her body, one arm holding it while the other kept her secure against the ladder. Paul quickly walked over and took the box from her.

"Oh, good morning, dearest," Lois greeted.

"Morning, love. What are you doing?"

"I thought we should start packing everything up now, since Winston will probably want to call the gas leak on Monday. The girls' suitcases are downstairs already, and there're a few rentable garages in Meadowstream for the rest. We can get one and put everything in there to keep it safe. And I have the key to Nancy's house, so we can get her and James' stuff as well."

Paul smiled.

"What?"

"You're a genius," he said seriously, and Lois laughed.

It only took them a few hours to get everything boxed up and ready to go, keeping it upstairs so that Paul's parents wouldn't see it and ask any uncomfortable questions. They were just sitting down when the doorbell rang, and Lois sprang up to answer it with Paul on her heels.

"Paul! Lois! Hello!" Heather greeted, giving them both a hug. James was right behind them, giving them both a hug right after his wife.

"How are you?" James asked.

"We're good, dad. We just remembered how long it's been

150

since the kids saw you, and thought we'd see if you wanted to host them for a few days while me and Lois had some time to ourselves."

"It was a very good idea!" Heather exclaimed, and Lois chuckled.

"I'm glad you think so."

"Oh, but we don't see *you* enough, Lois. Did I ever tell you how glad I am that Paul married you?"

"Oh, at least once," Lois replied, and Heather laughed.

It was strange to casually entertain someone in the midst of a situation like theirs, but such normalcy was appreciated. Lois was just glad she hadn't had another situation of time splitting apart, or anyone being reset to how they were before she'd seen them.

"The kids should be here about now," Lois said, getting up and walking out the door in time to see her children leaving Nancy's backyard. Maureen and Jane were talking with them, so Lois brought all of them inside. Once Heather and James saw them, Lois was free to walk back outside—Paul following close behind.

"Where are you going?" He asked in as casual a voice as he could manage.

"I'm going to tell Nancy that your parents are here, and so are her kids," Lois replied as they stepped into Nancy's yard.

"Ah. I'll join you."

He linked their arms as they walked up the stairs onto Nancy's porch and knocked on the door.

"Hold on a minute, girls!" Nancy called out, and a few seconds later she opened the door looking like she'd just run a marathon.

"Girls, you look so different," Nancy joked, her tone only slightly unsure.

Paul chuckled.

"Maureen and Jane are next door with their grandparents. What on Earth are you doing?"

"Packing, what does it look like?"

It seemed Nancy had the same idea—most of her family's belongings were packed up in boxes and bags. It appeared

151

she'd started after the girls went to play outside, counting on them not coming back in.

"Once I finished I was going to tell Heather and James that I just needed to have a few things dropped off somewhere," She explained before either of them could ask how she planned to move to a new house before leaving to go up to her parent in laws' house.

"We actually did something similar," Paul told her, and Lois added, "Nancy, me and Paul are bringing our belongings to a garage. We can bring your things there as well, and you and James can go with our parents without making them too curious."

Nancy wiped her hands on her pants before hugging Lois and patting her on the shoulder.

"You're always thinking ahead, Lois. Thank you."

"Can we help you with the rest?" Paul asked, and Nancy graciously accepted their aid; within ten minutes the remainder of the other McCarthy family's belongings were ready to go.

"We should probably go back over before they start to wonder where we are," Lois said once her hair was fixed back up, and the three of them headed to Lois and Paul's with all of Nancy's family's suitcases in tow.

The younger James arrived a few minutes after they finished packing, seeing his parents' car in Lois and Paul's driveway and heading there without stopping in his house. Nancy murmured the plan to James and he agreed, briefly disappearing to make sure they'd gotten everything before coming back and convincing Heather and James Sr. that it was best they get going.

Maureen and Jane climbed into their parent's car as James Jr. put all their suitcases in the trunk and Nancy started the car. James Sr. started his car and Heather climbed in while Paul put his childrens' suitcases in the trunk. Lois stood close by, Mary and Linda each holding one of her hands. Mary's other hand was nervously clutching the strap of her backpack, her teddy bear held in the crook of her arm.

"It's only for the weekend," Lois assured Mary, who

sniffed slightly and nodded.

"You'll have Linda right with you, and your grandparents, and your aunt and uncle, *and* your cousins."

Mary giggled at Lois's intonation and Lois smiled before pulling both of her daughters into a hug.

"We're just a phone call away," Paul added as he closed the trunk to the car and joined into the group hug.

"Auntie Nancy and Uncle James will drive you back down here on Monday, okay?"

The girls nodded.

"Alright. We love you."

"To the moon and back."

Lois and Paul let go and both gave each of their daughters a hug and a kiss before helping them climb into the car. Lois helped Linda, turning to her quietly.

"How were you feeling in the dead of night?"

"Like the jokers in a deck," Linda murmured in response, and Lois kissed her daughter on the forehead and squeezed her hands before standing back up.

"Wait! Before we leave, I forgot to give this to you, mommy!" Mary exclaimed just as Lois was about to close the car door.

"Oh? What is it, Mary?" She asked, and Mary pulled off her backpack and pulled out a piece of thick paper with newspaper and magazine clippings glued onto it.

"The collage! We got them back on Friday, but I forgot! Here, mommy, doesn't that lady in the purple dress look like you?"

Lois took the collage and glanced at it, stiffening when she noticed the lady in question.

It was her.

The model, wearing a lavender dress and smiling out at her, was her.

Lois managed to keep her expression pleasant, though Paul noticed what Mary didn't.

"Oh, she *does*, Mary, what a coincidence!" Mary smiled as Paul came around to Lois's side and looked at the collage his wife handed to him, turning so that his kids couldn't see his expression.

"Alright, goodbye, Mary, goodbye, Linda. We'll see you in a few days, and we love you!" Lois said.

"Very much!" Paul added, composing himself before turning back.

"I love you!" Both girls replied, and Lois closed the door.

They waved until both cars were out of sight before quickly hurrying into their house.

Chapter 19

"That's you. That's—that's you in the advert!" Paul stammered, and Lois nodded. He was less used to this, but both of them were on edge. Lois quickly took both of his hands as he blinked and tried to process this.

"Darling. Look at me. Look at me. Okay? It's okay. Once everything's gone, this will all be over."

Paul slowly nodded, consciously slowing his breathing. Lois pulled him into a hug and he returned it tightly, staying together until he was felt like he was steady on his feet.

Lois called Harold—needing to do so twice, as he was not at his shop—and discovered that he was alone at his house, packing.

"There's a few garages over in the next town, and we wanted to know if we could use your pickup to bring all of our and Nancy's things over to it."

"I already reserved a few, we can bring them all to the same place. Gather all your stuff in one house and I'll come over after I've brought all of my things over there. And call Winston so he does the same."

"Okay. Thanks, Harry."

"See you soon, Lois." Harold hung up and Lois turned to Paul and told him what Harold had said, though Paul's head had been so close to the phone that he'd heard most of it.

Lois called Winston, who was thankfully at his house as well.

"Have you packed everything up too?" Lois asked first.

"Just about. What is it?"

"Harry rented some garages in the next town over and we're going to be bringing all of our things there. He said to call you so you can have it ready to bring over there as well."

A laugh.

"The man's on top of it, I see. I'll have everything ready in about two hours, maybe two and a half."

"Alright. He's bringing his things over first and then coming to help us, but we're also bringing Nancy and James's things, and there's the furniture, so you have time."

Winston whistled.

"I see. Alright, good. Has—has anything happened to you today?"

Lois described the collage.

"Freaky, but nothing too big. That's good. We can talk about what you heard at the meeting later. Goodbye."

"Goodbye."

Harold came over about half an hour after they'd called him, just as they'd finished moving Nancy's things and packed up the remainder of their belongings.

"This is going to take multiple trips," he told them upon seeing all the boxes.

"That's fine. As long as we can get them out of here," Paul responded, and Lois nodded in agreement. All three of them put as many packages as they could in Harold's truck bed, piling them up before covering them with a secured tarp.

"Only two people can fit in the front seat," Harold said once they were ready to go, and Paul and Lois immediately looked at each other.

"Paul, you're stronger. You go and I'll make sure nothing happens here," She insisted, and Paul was about to argue when Harold said casually, "She's right, you know."

A sharp glance was directed at the mechanic, but it was Paul and Harold who drove off.

Lois busied herself with reorganising the remaining boxes, but within a few minutes they were as ready to go as she'd be able to get them. Lois sighed and went into the fridge, taking out the flask of orange juice and pouring herself a glass. She sat down and glanced at the collage left on the table, staring at her own face as she took a sip.

Lois immediately spat the juice out, coughing and sticking her tongue out of her mouth; the viscous orange liquid dripped from her lips and splattered onto the table top. Her teeth scraped her tongue as she got up and ran the tap, sticking

156

her head down to wash out her mouth.

Instead of orange juice, the liquid had been egg yolk.

Lois went to pour out the flask, but as she was holding it over the sink she realised she could smell oranges. She tilted the container and the juice moved freely, revealing how thin it was. With a tentative sip, Lois identified it as orange juice— the glass flask fell from her hands and shattered in the sink, all of the liquid quickly draining away.

With a shaking hand she put her glass in the sink and took a rag to wipe off the table, eyes wide and breath sharp. Once it was clean she busied herself going upstairs and dismantling the furniture that was too big to transport.

Paul and Harold returned a short time later, Paul immediately able to tell that something had happened.

"I, I just sat down to pour myself something to drink. But when I drank some of it, it wasn't orange juice, it was egg yolk. I, I went to pour it out, but it was orange juice again. I dropped it—it broke in the sink."

Both of them took a look, Paul then checking Lois's hands to make sure she hadn't somehow cut herself. Her hands were slightly roughed by working with the wood of their furniture but otherwise unhurt.

"Alright. Well, we can fit all these in for a second trip, and then I'll come back for the furniture. And I can go alone." Harold said, and Paul nodded, giving his wife a quick hug before they went and packed up Harold's truck again.

As he drove away, Lois and Paul were left in a mostly empty house. They quickly busied themselves by dismantling the remainder of the furniture.

"At least it was still something edible," Paul mused as they took apart the couch.

"Unexpected, but yes. I—it could be anything. Anything could be anything."

Paul was unsure if he was more unsettled by the implication of his wife's statement or the resigned, quietly fearful way she'd said it.

"We'll be out of here soon. All of our things will be gone by today, and then Winston can call the gas leak. Everyone should be out by Tuesday, and then we can fix this and go." Paul assured her, and she nodded. Privately, however, she was still on an edge she'd been on for days; how could she be sure that they'd be able to fix anything when she couldn't trust her eyes?

Nothing too unusual happened by the time Harold returned; a few of the pieces of Nancy and James's furniture had moved back to that house, but they'd located everything as the truck drove up.

"It really does feel different as you leave town," Harold informed them as they packed the furniture up, playing what felt like a full dimensional puzzle game to get as much of it in at once.

"It's like a weight has been lifted. The energy here has been getting steadily worse." Usually everyone ignored when Harold said things like that, but Paul nodded.

"I noticed that too. A little," he admitted, and Harold gave him a small smile.

"Well, at least you're finally paying attention."

Lois and Paul were again left alone as Harold left, promising them that they'd be able to fit everything left for one last trip when he returned. This time they sat out on their now empty porch, right next to each other on the stairs. They spotted Winston putting some boxes on his porch and waved, getting up and walking across the street as he beckoned them over.

"I've got almost everything ready. Was that your last trip for Harry?"

"We've only got one more. Just the rest of the furniture." Winston nodded.

"Alright. Has anything else happened?"

Lois told him about the egg yolk incident and Paul added that some of Nancy and James's furniture had teleported back into their house.

"I had that problem. I had to take apart me and Cyn's bed three times." Winston was clearly shaken. Lois put a hand on his arm while Paul patted his shoulder.

"I'm going to call the gas leak tonight. Give everyone time

go get out."

Paul and Lois nodded.

"Good idea."

"It'll only get worse," Lois added.

Winston gritted his teeth.

"We should stay together after this. All in one house, or one place." It sounded more like an order than a suggestion.

"Once Harry's back we can decide where."

The three proceeded to pack up or dismantle the rest of Winston's belongings, finishing just as Harold pulled into Lois and Paul's driveway. They hurried across the street to greet him, Winston right behind them.

"We can stay at the garage," Harold decided after Winston told him the plan.

"Any particular reason?" He asked as they packed the truck.

"Everything seems to be worse in the neighborhood. Almost everything that's happened to Lois has been here. Everything froze everywhere, and the park aside, all the other things seem to be centralised to the neighborhood and not the town."

The others could not argue with this, so they agreed to go to the garage once their things were all gone.

"There's a phone there, too, so we can still call people," Harold told them, seeing Paul tucking his telephone inside a drawer.

Lois and Paul waited with Winston as Harold drove back and forth from the garage, slowly taking all of his things. Once everything was gone and Harold was off on the last trip they were left sitting on the steps of Winston's porch, silent and sober.

"I can't believe it's been eight years," Lois said quietly, staring at her garden across the street. Paul put his arm around her and pulled her a little closer to him.

"Linda was only a year old when we came here." His tone was dreamy and distracted.

"I've been here for twelve," Winston said absently, fiddling with his hands.

"Jules was three and May was two. I got transferred here from a state over. Me and Cyn had been in that house for years before we came here—I remember that she didn't want to move. Then she grew to love this house, even more than the old one. Now she's insisting we leave as soon as possible."

Winston scoffed and kicked a rock off the steps.

"I never would have imagined something like this happening. I thought this move would be permanent."

"Me too," Paul and Lois said in unison.

They stared back forwards in silence.

All three of them fell into their own thoughts, caught up in a reverie when Lois was distracted by something in the corner of her eye. She looked away from her garden to see the world was not as it seemed.

"Do. Do you see that?" She asked in a shaky, quiet voice, pulling Paul and Winston from their thoughts. They glanced at Lois before looking in the direction she was staring: Nancy's house, at a glance, appeared normal. However, upon looking closer it became apparent that something was…off.

"What *is* that?" Winston asked, leaning forward a bit and squinting through his glasses. Paul and Lois instinctively reached for each other's hands as they stared at…whatever it was.

Between the door and one of the windows of Nancy's house there was a line of some kind. A fold, glimmering slightly if it was stared at for long enough to observe it. It looked like someone had folded a sheet of laminated paper, leaving a visible seam. The house bent slightly around it, the window and door leaning ever so slightly towards it.

"It's just…"

"Bent." Paul and Lois said. Winston made a deep, guttural sound of disbelief. As the three of them looked around, they realised that the seams were everywhere; the entirety of their visible surroundings gave the appearance of a stitched storybook. All three of them leapt off the porch and stumbled together into the yard, turning to see that there was one right in the middle of Winston's door.

"What do we do?" Lois asked.

"Don't touch it," Winston said immediately.

"*Other* than the obvious," she replied.

Winston reached over for the rock he'd kicked off the porch steps. The three of them were arm to arm as Winston slowly wound back and threw the rock at his front door, hitting the seam head on.

Three pairs of eyes widened as they stared at the rock. Instead of bouncing off and falling to the ground, it had frozen right in the middle of the seam. They inched forwards until they were just a few feet away, right at the bottom of the steps—the rock was visibly bending inwards, folding with the seam as if it had been drawn smack dab in the middle of a book.

"What the hell?" Winston wondered aloud.

Lois and Paul were grasping at each other as Winston slowly stepped onto the first stair, his hand trembling as he held it halfway up.

"Don't." Lois said sharply, and Winston glanced back to see both of them shaking their heads.

Harold drove up to see the three of them staring intently at Winston's door. He stepped out of the truck and stared for a moment before coughing. All three of them jumped, Winston falling back into Paul and Lois and knocking all of them over.

"Christ, what's scared you all? What happened while I was gone?" Harold asked as he hurried over to the pile of his friends. Three fingers immediately pointed at the door, which Harold turned to look at.

"What?"

The three of them untangled themselves and sat up to see that the seam was gone. They leapt up and looked around in disbelief, but all the seams were gone. The world was normal again, the rock sitting directly in front of the door.

"There were these, these folds!" Paul managed to say first.

"Seams, seams in the air, in front of people's houses—like, like the fold in the middle of a book, they, they were bending things, we—" Lois stuttered.

Winston interrupted, "I threw that rock at it and it just

stayed there, floating in the air, bending in the fold! I don't know when it stopped. Right as we turned around. They were everywhere, in front of everyone's houses."

Harold held up his hands to stop them from trying to explain it any further.

"Alright. Come on, one of you get in the front and the other two jump in the truck bed, we're going to the garage."

They all nodded. After a brief discussion, Lois was sitting in the front with Harold, Paul and Winston sitting in the back of the truck right by the back window.

"Are you alright?" Harold asked as he pulled out of Winston's driveway and headed for town.

"I think so," Lois replied quietly. Even the golden light of the sinking sun wasn't enough to warm the colour of her face.

"I've gotten slightly used to it, as horrible as that sounds."

"It's better that it doesn't freeze you up. You've got to be on your toes. You seem to be the only one who isn't forgetting anything," Harold assured her.

There was a slight pause.

"How can we be sure of that?" she asked in a shaking whisper.

"We can't. But we can be sure that what you have seen is right, and that you're helping everyone."

Lois, Winston, and Paul were shocked to see how empty the shop was. It was impossible to tell from outside, but the whole interior had been cleaned out.

"I moved everything I could yesterday and this morning," he explained as they passed through the empty office and went back upstairs. A phone, two old stuffed chairs, a lamp, a few books, the desk, and the original worn couch were the only things that occupied the space now.

"Figured Paul and Lois could share the couch," Harold drawled, saying just enough to explain the whole sleeping situation as he handed each of them a key to the office door. Now they could let themselves in and out of the building.

"Alright. I've got to get to the station. The cruiser's there, I'll walk," Winston said, "I already broke a few pipes outside of empty houses, made it look like they burst. I'll send some

162

of the probies around and tell them I've gotten calls about people who think there's a gas leak. They'll buy it, and I'll call it tonight."

Once Winston was gone the remaining three got settled. The sun was practically gone and stars were beginning to become visible through the loft window. Harold made himself comfortable in one of the sofa chairs and occupied himself with a book while Lois and Paul laid down on the couch, Lois practically on top of Paul to keep from falling. Both of them were exhausted from moving boxes all day, but even as they closed their eyes and laid still neither of them was able to fall asleep.

The phone rang and Lois and Paul jumped enough to fall off the couch, Harold calmly reaching over and picking up the receiver.

"Harold's Garage. Harold speaking," he greeted. Lois and Paul stared up, frozen on the floor.

"Good to hear. Alright. Will do. See you soon."

He put the receiver down and glanced at Lois and Paul, who scrambled to get back on the couch.

"Winston says they bought the gas leak, and a few of the cops actually fainted due to apparent gas exposure. He called the evacuation and told his underlings that he'd call the garage himself. He said he'll be here in about an hour or so, when he can get away without raising any questions."

Lois and Paul blinked.

"Do you think they just thought there was gas and somehow reacted?" Paul asked.

"I don't think so. With the way you two were talking, I wouldn't be too surprised if there really is gas there now." Harold replied, and Lois took a sharp breath.

"It probably won't end up here," Harold immediately assured her, but the uncertainty of the situation put them all on edge.

Winston let himself in and came upstairs to find Harold trying to read a book and Lois and Paul sitting on the couch staring at nothing.

"Everyone's leaving en masse," he announced, everyone

turning to look at him. The sound of cars was audible even with the windows closed.

"They should all be gone by tomorrow. We might be able to do this even earlier than we thought. Some of the boys are staying in the next town over so they can oversee the evacuation, and tomorrow I'll send them out to make sure everyone's out before telling them to get out of town. I said tonight that I was having some feds come to check on the leaks, so they don't want any part of it."

"What is the plan, exactly?" Lois asked as Winston sunk into the remaining chair.

"Some of the boys measured some actual gas levels, so this might be easier than I thought. We can't use non-gaseous accelerants because those might be found and the town might be put under suspicion of mass arson. My idea is to light a few of the houses and see if it catches, and if not, spread it ourselves. Once enough of the houses catch it'll grow on its own, since the houses are close enough together and all the fences are wood. The town will be a bit harder, since some of the buildings have more stone and metal, but it shouldn't be too difficult."

Paul and Lois exchanged glances, Harold closing his book and turning off the lamp.

"Well. We'd better get some sleep."

Chapter 20

Harold fell asleep first, followed by Winston. Paul knew Lois was awake when he eventually drifted off, grip still secure around her as she was left alone. Lois's body was exhausted, but her mind was racing; she had never even gotten a parking ticket, let alone burnt down an entire town. A town that they were *fairly* sure was causing all this—but not positive. That uncertainty was eating at Lois more than all the other ones. She couldn't trust her eyes or her ears and now she couldn't even trust if committing arson and burning down her home of eight years would solve the problems plaguing them.

Lois's eyes blinked open when a strange light became apparent. She squinted, seeing that it was coming from the window—sunlight. Even without a clock, Lois knew it wasn't morning yet; she'd only lied down about an hour ago. Lois stared as her eyes got used to the light—she could see stars. Untangling herself from Paul's grip, she stood up and walked over to the window, slowly opening it and sticking her head outside.

The sky was a brilliant pinkish red, orange clouds spread amongst the stars. Staring in the direction of the neighborhood, Lois could see the skies stretching all the way as far as she could see, the moon hanging over the houses. It was only when she turned that she froze in place: night was visible. Harold's garage was on the very edge of Rose Park, near the road that lead to the nearest town. Right over the town line, the light stopped and darkness was visible beyond. Lois blinked. It was nothing like she'd ever seen.

"Lois?" A sleepy voice asked from behind her. She turned to see her absence had woken Paul.

"Come take a look at this."

Her husband rose and stumbled over to stand next to her at the window. His eyes, too, widened in shock as he stared at the sky. Eventually he also spotted the border where night was falling elsewhere. Cars were racing out of Rose Park and into the darkness, the stragglers clearly terrified by what they were seeing.

"By the stars. What the hell are we seeing?" Paul asked rhetorically as he took his wife's hand.

"At least everyone will probably think they're hallucinating because of the gas," Lois murmured.

"I wish that was what was happening," Paul responded, tugging lightly at Lois as he turned to head back to the couch. She turned and followed but paused.

"Where's the light gone?" Lois asked, worry creeping into her voice, and they looked back over their shoulders. The sky, again, was a black blanket of stars.

Lois and Paul did not get any more sleep that night.

Harold woke up a little before the sun was actually supposed to rise, upset but not surprised to see Lois and Paul half sitting up and awake. They immediately told him about what they'd seen.

"The whole sky?" Harold asked, and Lois and Paul shook their heads.

"It ended where the town did. Beyond that it was like it is now, the sky pitch black like it's supposed to be," Lois explained. The idle chatter woke Winston, who was told the story immediately upon reaching full consciousness.

Winston reached over for the phone and dialed the station, the phone ringing a few times before being picked up.

"It's Chief Johnson," Winston said before they could give the regular spiel, "Who's in the station right now? Alright, that's enough. I want you all to go out and make sure everyone is evacuated. *Everyone*. Once you know they're all gone get back to the station and call me. I'm at Harold's garage, so don't bother checking here and use that number. Alright? Good. Go."

It was a tense hour before the phone rang again and the officer reported that the town was empty.

"Good. Excellent job. The feds should be here shortly, so all of you get out and go to wherever you're staying. Yes. I'll be getting out soon, and I'll handle the feds. Yes. Yes. Alright. Thank you. Goodbye." He hung up the phone with a sigh.

"Let's drive back to my house. I left a few things in the basement we can use—the boys will be out by the time we're ready."

They all piled into the truck, Winston and Paul in the back like before as they headed into town. There was certainly a slight smell, but Harold had thought ahead and provided them all with clean rags they wore like bandanas to cover their noses and mouths. They stopped in front of Winston's house, jumping out and following him through the door and down into the basement. There they found that he'd somehow gotten a hold of dozens of cans of hairspray, bottles of nail polish, various alcoholic drinks, and acetone nail polish remover. All of them were stacked into boxes for transport.

"What, did you raid people's houses?" Lois asked.

"While we were having people be evacuated I went around and convinced some of them that I'd be getting rid of things that weren't necessary to travel with. Turns out a lot of them were willing to give this up," Winston explained, picking up a box and encouraging the others to do the same. They eventually had all eight boxes in the back of Harold's truck.

"Barbara's house is just about in the middle of the neighborhood. We'll start with hers."

They drove the short distance over. All four of them took a bottle of hairspray and emptied them in and around the house, coating everything and saturating the air with Helene Curtis's Spray Net. The less flammable items left in the house were coated with some of the acetone and nail polish to make it easier for them to keep the flames. A few bottles of cheap alcohol were left in places to feed the fire as they thought might be necessary.

All four of them stood back a good distance and stared at the house, faces screwing up at the stench of beauty products. They waited a few minutes for the spray to settle at Winston's suggestion, wanting to avoid the air around them catching flame and taking them out with the house. Eventually, Harold lit a match—when their surroundings didn't burn around them, he tossed it onto the porch steps. It didn't take more than a few seconds for the wood to take light.

The house was entirely engulfed in flames within seconds, but before the neighboring house could catch, the flames suddenly went still. Lois blinked, staring at the spectacle before turning to look at the others. They, too, were frozen in place.

Lois was beginning to reach her limit of things she could take. She tried to throw a can of hairspray at the fire, but the minute she let go of it the container froze in the middle of the air. In irritation, she grabbed it and put it back in the box she'd taken it from. Her hands ran through her hair, body trembling.

"How are we supposed to fix this if the rules keep changing?" she shouted, about to start screaming again when the crackling of fire and the sound of a glass bottle exploding from within the house became audible.

Lois turned to see that the house was burning again, but she was alone—Winston, Harold, and Paul were nowhere to be found. Harold's truck was gone, but the boxes of incendiaries remained. Lois numbly moved the boxes into the street where they wouldn't be likely to catch fire and walked to her house, pulling her keys out of her pocket and opening the garage. She got into her car and drove to the garage, discovering that they weren't there, either. In fact, as she drove around, she discovered that the entirety of Rose Park was deserted.

Lois was alone.

After parking the car on the side of the road out of town, Lois walked all the way back to Barbara's house. It took her quite a while, but a quiet determination had filled her body and made her numb to the pain in her feet and knees from the distance. Barbara's house was half gone and the two neighboring homes had caught light, though they were burning slower due to the lack of added fuel. Lois took one of the boxes and went across the street, picking a random house and soaking it full of hairspray and acetone.

Hours passed as Lois slowly went from random house to random house. It was getting harder to move, the world seeming to warp around her; Lois's heart was pounding as she witnessed houses switching positions, flames of all different colours stretching as smoke filled the air. The sky grew darker and darker as Lois dragged herself through the neighborhood, the rag not enough to protect her from all of the smoke.

A high-pitched noise filled the air as she reached town and spread the fire onwards, taking special care to soak buildings that had a lot of brick and metal. The air was getting hot and heavy as she headed for the road that would bring her back to her car and out of town, but a nagging feeling stopped her in her tracks. She turned back in the direction of the neighborhood, everything smouldering and smoking in the thick air.

Something was off.

The sound of crying and a flash of familiar hair was visible running through the smoke into the residential area. Lois dropped the box she was carrying and ran after it, her breathing dangerously fast and her heart beating so loudly she could hear it over the increasingly loud screaming in the air.

Lois followed the sound of sobbing through the cloud of smoke, eventually coming to her own house. The flames seemed unable to touch this area—as Lois stepped onto her yard she was greeted with fresh, clean air. Sunlight touched her dirty skin as she stared at her porch.

Linda.

Lois's eldest daughter was standing on the porch, looking scared. She was coated in ashes and rubbing at red eyes, her body shaking. Lois immediately ran up to her, wrapping her arms around her.

"Linda, it's okay, I'm here. I'm here," Lois assured her. They sat down on the steps together, Lois kissing her daughter in between thick coughs. Linda tightly gripped her mother, sniffing and crying into Lois's shoulder.

Distracted by her daughter, it took Lois several minutes to notice what was happening around her. Instead of the fire encroaching upon them, it was receding back—Nancy's house, which had been burning when Lois had stepped onto her yard, was in pristine condition again. Glancing around, Lois saw that there was a sphere of restoration that was slowly spreading forwards. Lois had to burn her house down or all her work was going to be for nothing.

"Linda, we have to go now, sweetie," Lois murmured, trying to stand up. Linda's grip became heavier and she kept sitting, making it difficult for Lois to get to her feet.

"Linda, please. We have to get out of here."

"But it's safe here! There's no fire!" Linda retorted.

"Linda, it won't stay that way. We have to go. We have to let the house burn."

"No!"

Lois managed to pick Linda up and had started walking towards the sidewalk when the child wrestled out of her mother's grip and ran back to the porch steps.

"I won't let you!" Linda shouted, backing up against the front door. Lois paused, staring at her daughter. She swallowed hard, thinking clearly even through the smoke that had affected her and slowed her. Lois's hands reached into the pockets of her apron, feeling around for the bottles of nail polish and liquor she'd tucked into them earlier when she started carrying the boxes herself.

"Linda, how were you feeling in the dead of night?" Lois asked, looking right into her daughter's eyes. Linda looked back, her expression adamant and frightened.

"Like the jokers in a deck."

Lois felt like someone had punched her in the chest. That was the phrase she and Linda had agreed upon, but…how had Linda gotten back to Rose Park? How could she have? A few tears burned at Lois's eyes but her grip on the bottles tightened.

"Linda, we have to go. Now." Lois's voice was stern, but Linda did not budge.

"Linda!"

"No!" Linda insisted, staring angrily at her mother. Lois closed her eyes for a moment. How was she supposed to do this? She looked around again, seeing the fire getting further and further away. Everything was going to be reset again. What if people started popping up too? Lois couldn't bear thinking about what would happen if her neighbors were zapped back to Rose Park just in time to be burnt to cinders. She had to do this now.

Lois pulled a bottle of whiskey out of her pocket and threw it at the house, watching it shatter as it came into contact with the door. Linda winced and cried out, Lois feeling physical pain at the sound but still throwing a bottle of nail polish after it, flinching as it crashed through the window and showered the girl with glass.

"Mom, stop!" Linda shouted, fear thick in her voice. Lois's hands shook as she took the matches out of her pocket, tears pouring down her face. She stared at what looked just like her daughter. She *knew* it wasn't her Linda, but...

"Mom, please! *Please!*" Linda begged, sobbing and collapsing to her knees.

"Linda, if you just come with me, you'll be safe." Lois found herself saying, unable to stop the words from coming out of her mouth. There was no point in asking. Linda shook her head.

Lois swallowed the gigantic lump in her throat and closed her eyes. She heard herself strike the match and threw it.

"*NO!*"

Lois collapsed to her knees as screams erupted from the house, screeching cries that sounded *just like Linda.*

The smoke surrounding Lois flooded in as she sobbed on her lawn, body shaking and numbing as the screaming became less and less human. She opened her eyes and they stung, a hand managing to cover the cloth on her face as the smoke choked her. With great difficulty Lois rose to her feet, staring at her home as it burned for a few more moments.

Lois turned and ran as fast as she could, heading blindly back for town. The columns of flames were rising around her, the air getting hotter and thicker with black, the inhuman screaming reaching a painful volume. She could feel her skin burning as her body got slower, her head swimming and her lungs seizing as she coughed more than she could breathe.

She fell to her hands and knees and crawled forwards, reaching the town and heading desperately for the edge of it. She couldn't even see any landmarks through the thick flames and the heavy smoke, having to rely on the feeling of concrete below her blistering hands as she was blinded. After what felt like hours, each second harder than the last, Lois finally reached the edge of town.

The second her entire body had left Rose Park Lois's world went black and she collapsed.

Chapter 21

Lois could barely hear it at first, but something was getting louder and louder.

"Lois!" The voice finally said in a way she could interpret. "Lois! *Lois!*"

Lois opened her eyes to find that they were not burning—in fact, none of her was. She felt fine…better than she had before, even. Lois looked up to see that Paul was bending over her, eyes wide. He broke out into a smile upon her seeing him, pulling her into a hug.

Looking over his shoulder she could see that she was in a building she didn't recognise. Patricia, Harold, Nancy, James, Eleanor, Brian, Barbara, Richard, Cynthia, and Winston were all gathered in the room around her. As she blinked, she realised she could hear the sound of young children and babies babbling and crying.

Barbara was quietly crying, Eleanor holding her hand as she sniffed.

"What happened?" Lois asked, and Paul leaned back so he could look at her. Lois blinked and her eyes widened.

"Paul! You look—"

"Young?" he asked, and she nodded; Paul appeared to be at least a decade younger, any wrinkles or stray grays he'd had gone. Lois looked around to see that all of them were younger than they had been, some more noticeably than others.

Paul helped Lois sit up on the couch she was lying on, taking a seat next to her.

"About an hour ago now, we all found ourselves on the edge of Meadowstream. We noticed pretty immediately that we were younger, but it took a little while for us to work it out. We're all the age we were before we moved to Rose Park. Me and you are eight years younger, Winston and

Cynthia are twelve years younger, and so on."

Lois blinked, but before she could ask anything, Paul continued, "You were the only one who didn't appear with us. While the others reserved this motel room, me, Winston, and Harry drove out in Harry's truck in the direction of Rose Park. We found you passed out right next to where the town line was, a few yards away from our car. It's...its gone."

Lois's eyebrows furrowed, but she couldn't find any words. That was a lot to take in.

"There's not even cinders left. Rose Park isn't even how it was years ago. And it would seem we've gone back even further than some of us thought," Winston added. Lois turned to him with saucer eyes. Cynthia, younger than Lois could ever remember, held out a newspaper. Lois looked down at it and her breath hitched in her throat.

The year was 1946—ten years ago.

"None of the other townsfolk ended up here. It would seem, for some reason, it's just us." Nancy told her. Lois looked up at her, phased by how young her sister in law looked. She was barely older than her now. Eleanor saw her staring and handed her a compact, allowing Lois to look at herself. She stared openly, eyes wide at the lack of wrinkles, the brightness of skin, the time wound back and bringing her to her early twenties.

"The girls," Lois said, Eleanor catching the compact with her free hand as it fell from her grip.

"The girls—"

"Lois, we weren't the only ones affected." Paul's voice was soft and sober.

Lois turned to him and he got up, walking over to the other side of the room where all the sounds were coming from. He reached over in the crowd of children and lifted up a little girl that was just barely a toddler. Lois gasped gently as Paul carried her over, placing her on Lois's lap.

It was Linda, as she had been eight years ago—just a year old.

"We haven't had Mary yet." He explained quietly as Lois wrapped her arms around Linda, the little girl cooing and babbling as she held onto her mother.

Lois was hit by a shock of emotion, caught between the shock of the situation and the horror at the fact that she'd just lost a child. Linda grasped hold of her thumb.

A few calls later, Harold ascertained that all their things were gone. They were the only ones affected by the reset, all of them going back to the way they'd been before Rose Park had caught them. Barbara and Eleanor had lost one child each, the remaining offspring too young to comprehend the situation. Lois and Paul's things were still in their old apartment. Everyone else had a similar story, Winston learning in frustration that all of his and Cynthia's things were in their old house a whole state over. The silver lining was they still had their things, but no amount of news like that could absolve the feeling they all had; a unique sensation of group isolation.

Lois and Paul were finally alone hours and hours later, after they had all exchanged numbers and the others had left to go home. Lois and Paul got into their car, Paul getting in the driver's seat and Lois sitting shotgun with a sleepy Linda on her lap. They were headed back to their apartment, dimly aware they'd have to look for a new house again. Lois gently stroked Linda's hair and stared out the window, still processing the situation.

"Can you show me what's there?" Lois asked, Paul not needing to ask what she meant.

"Of course."

He turned off the main way and they drove through gravelly roads until they came to the very edge of Rose Park. Lois stepped out of the car with Linda in her arms, seeing the tire tracks where she'd had the car right off what was a real road ten years into a voided future.

Paul got out and walked to her side as she slowly approached the edge of—nothing. The entirety of Rose Park, instead of being the small town it was supposed to be when Winston had been there, was a huge open field. Lois stepped over the barrier and immediately felt the weight on her shoulders again.

She stared for a long time, thoughts hitting her consciousness at high speed.

"Are you ready to go, dear?" Paul asked after a while. Lois turned to him. He hadn't stepped over the barrier, hadn't started to feel what she had. Instead, he was looking at her with soft eyes, expression tired but hopeful. To him, it was over.

Lois smiled, and he smiled back.

"Yes."

Lois stepped off of Rose Park and felt the heaviness go. Paul smiled and pulled her over to him, leaning in to kiss her.

They climbed back into the car and Lois stared forwards at Rose Park as Paul looked backwards in order to properly turn the car. Her smile faltered slightly, but she sighed.

Lois felt calm.

It was over for Paul, and it was over for her. It was over. As they drove away, Lois looked at the car's side mirror and watched the land disappear behind them. It was *over*.

Right?

DID YOU ENJOY WHAT YOU JUST READ?

If you enjoyed this book, *please* review it on Amazon and GoodReads!

It's the best way to support the author.

For fantastic fiction, in-depth articles by your favourite authors, open submissions, and more, please…

VISIT OUR WEBSITE
18thwall.com/

LIKE US ON FACEBOOK
facebook.com/18thwall/

FOLLOW US ON TWITTER
@18thWall

We'd love to hear from you! You help make these books possible.

Author Bio

Anna Maloney has been writing all her life, but *Every Little Thing* is her first published novel. As a time travel enthusiast who is so often looking at the past, her debut book does fittingly encapsulate two of her biggest interests—the 1950s and the manipulation of time. They always say to write what you know, though as far as anyone's aware, the only decades she's been to are the ones she'd normally live through.

Previews

Bel Nemeton

Jon Black

UNCOVERING MERLIN'S TOMB

A globe-trotting quest for the treasures of the historical Merlin.

From the Preditors and Editors Readers' Poll
Award-Winning Author Jon Black...

Carvings have been unearthed in the Middle East. They bear impossible names--Arthur and Merlin, albeit in a native transliteration. How did these names come so far? Do they imply the existence of a historical Arthur and Merlin? The scholars do what they always do. They arrange a press meeting.

But scholars aren't the only attendees. After heavily-armed mercenaries steal the stone, Dr. Vivian Cuinnsey is forced to work with Jake Booker, a self-professed treasure hunter. Can he be trusted? Or is he just one more force after Merlin's treasure for personal profit?

From the Middle East to the caves of Israel to German record rooms to Oxford's secret underworld, chase Vivian and Jake in their pursuit of Merlin's greatest treasure.

Prologue

The dream was over. Tears streaked down his wizened face as he surveyed the landscape. Bodies lie strewn throughout the Camlann Valley. Chill winds carried the stench of smoke and blood into his acute nostrils. He arrived too late, taking too long to escape the bewitching Nimue's imprisonment. His escape was a tale worthy of Arthur and his best knights, but it didn't matter. He had failed in his duty as his king's advisor, wizard, and friend.

In his mind, Myrddin saw how the battle unfolded, as surely as if he had been there. Without the benefit of his counsel and his knowledge of tactics learned from the old Romans, Arthur and his men had simply charged, trusting that valor and strength of arms alone could carry the day against the traitorous Mordred and his Saxon allies.

He envisioned Camelot's finest as they charged the Saxon's fluttering banners along the broad, flat valley. Recent rains swelled the ancient River Cam, threatening to flood its banks. As the king and his company advanced, their formations grew ragtag and discipline frayed. Caring only about being first into the fray, the men ignored the high ground on either side of them. And so they remained ignorant of the surprise Morgana and Mordred concealed there. Myrddin would have done the same had he been in Mordred's place. He shuddered at the thought.

Still, Arthur and his knights had turned the tables, won the battle, and destroyed themselves in the process. Britain's king lingered for several hours afterward, so Myrddin was told. But the old man had not reached the Camlann in time to say goodbye.

He could not believe Arthur was gone. Arthur, whom, as a swaddled infant, Myrddin had cradled in his arms and sang to. Before Uther. Before even Ygrayne. Gone. Now, Brittan was without her king, the foe vanquished, and Mordred no more. Myrddin did not know if Morgana numbered among the living or the dead. He hoped it didn't matter. Without Mordred, Morgana amounted to nothing. Didn't she? But there would be another wave of Saxons. As far as Myrddin could tell, there would *always* be another wave of Saxons.

"Myrddin."

He looked up, it was Cei. The solemn and sober knight numbered among the handful of Arthur's host not only to survive the battle but remain, mostly, unscathed.

"Is it done?" Myrddin asked, wiping the tears from his face. Cei nodded gravely. Myrddin noticed the wound to the knight's face. His cheek would always have a scar. It would match the one on his heart.

How strange that, at the end, it should come down to the two of them. There had been no love to lose between Myrddin and Cei. Neither made any secret of it. Myrddin found the old warrior tiresome, self-righteous, moralistic, and utterly mirthless. He could only imagine what Cei must think of him. Despite that, each man understood and trusted the other's unconditional love for Arthur. That had been enough to unite them.

Cei surveyed his surroundings, searching. "Bedwyr?"

Myrddin shook his head. "Not yet returned," he clarified, lest Cei should misunderstand him and fear another of their company had fallen. Cei had completed his task, as Myrddin knew he would. He hoped Bedwyr possessed the mettle for what he'd been assigned. The venerable cavalier reminded Myrddin more of a grandfatherly otter than a fearsome Knight of the Round Table. With his gentle voice and kind heart, Bedwyr deserved birth into a better time and place. And yet, they also gifted the knight a curious kind of power. Even dead-hearted Mordred had possessed a soft spot for Bedwyr.

Time moved in circles, Myrddin reflected. It had been the three of them, Cei, Bedwyr, and Myrddin, with Arthur at the beginning. And it was the three of them here, at the end. He had known it would be so. More years ago than Myrddin carried to count or admit, he had dreamed. The kind of dream that Bleys, his ancient mentor, taught him to always pay attention to. In his dream, Camelot burned. Stone. Mortar. The rock foundation itself. Everything consumed in flames. Camelot burned and it fell to the three of them to dispose of the ashes.

And so they had. His dream had come to pass.

Myrddin studied the knight, "What will you do now?"

Cei considered the question. "Stay here. Rally the others. Try to pick up the pieces. You?"

Myrddin, too, thought before answering. He plumbed the depths of logic and reason as well as his intuition for omens and portents. Though tempted by Cei's answer, he could not allow himself to go there. "Darkness descends upon this land," Myrddin pronounced, "and no man shall stop it. I shall walk the wide world searching for Arthur's spirit. And, if I do not find it, I shall simply go home."

"God be with you in your quest," Cei said.

"And the gods be with you in yours."

Chapter One

"Damn it," Vivian Cuinnsey swore at her computer. Once again the document she was preparing failed to format properly.

"Everything okay, Doc?" Grant, her graduate assistant, poked his head through the door.

"I'll get this. Eventually. It'll be fine."

That stretched the truth. Since becoming department chair last year, she had been immersed in a world of budgets, policies, and academic politics that bordered on vendettas. Keeping a department full of idiosyncratic Celtic Language scholars running was a full time job.

Then there was the graduate seminar she taught. Only one class, but an important one, complete with rubrics, lesson plans, and grading. Vivian thought the move from undergraduate to graduate studies was a bigger transition than going from high school to undergraduate. Both high school and undergraduate revolved around what you knew. Graduate school involved coming to terms with what you didn't know. A little acclimation went a long way in helping new graduate students adjust to that shift.

And, of course, Vivian functioned as her department's chief fundraiser and its public face—to the university's administration, alumni, and the world at large.

Now, she faced additional pressure from an impending meeting with an Irish-American CEO, who, having embraced his roots, was considering a sizable endowment to her department. The document which had frustrated Vivian all afternoon was part of her campaign to make the donation a reality.

Another half-hour resolved the formatting issue. Sending Grant home for the evening, Vivian also prepared to leave. Checking email once more before closing her laptop, she was surprised to find a message from Dr. Weldon Grassley, a venerable professor emeritus with her university's department of archeology. Well past retirement age, Grassley remained on the university's payroll and perpetually in the field at excavations throughout Central Asia.

"Dear Vivian, I found this at an excavation in Uzbekistan. I would be very interested in your thoughts."

The attached photo showed a stele, an upright stone plinth, bearing inscriptions in three alphabets. She did not recognize the top two. The first was all thick shapes and dramatic lines. Thin loops and lines characterized the second. At the bottom, however, Vivian found the familiar Latin script she encountered a thousand times a day, the letters used by English and dozens of other languages.

Though uncertain why Grassley sent the photo to her, it piqued Vivian's interest. Greek inscriptions, courtesy of Alexander the Great, were sometimes found that far east. Latin was another matter entirely. A glance told her that, while the script was Latin, the language it recorded certainly wasn't. That came as no surprise. Many peoples had borrowed the script of the far-reaching Romans for recording languages not previously written. Excluding the cumbersome Ogham script, that included her beloved Celts.

Unraveling the Latin script's phonetics, Vivian saw familiar patterns. They were far better suited to the tongues of long ago Britain, Ireland, and Gaul than to the dusty caravan routes of Central Asia. The inscription seemed to be some form of Insular Celtic, the language family to which all living Celtic languages belonged. The words preserved on the stone stele manifested distinctly Insular Celtic traits like verb-subject-object word order and inflected prepositions. At the same time, they lacked traits associated with the other branch of Celtic, the now extinct Continental Celtic family, such as a third gender form.

Having determined the inscription to be Insular Celtic,

Vivian's next task was deciding to which of that family's two sub-branches it belonged. The Brittonic language family, still called "Brythonic" by some older linguists, included modern Breton, Cornish, and Welsh as well as their parent languages and a half-dozen extinct linguistic dead-ends. The Goidelic family of languages included modern Irish, Scottish, and Manx, all of which evolved from Middle Irish.

Dr. Grassley's inscription gave every indication of being Brittonic, specifically the tongue called "Common Brittonic." Between the fifth and seventh centuries, that language held sway from Scotland's River Clyde to France's Brittany Peninsula. After the Romans left Britain, distinct dialects of Common Brittonic began to emerge. Those dialects would one day become the separate languages of Breton, Cornish, and Welsh. Perhaps Cumbrian and Pictish, too. Opinions differed as to whether Cumbrian represented a distinct language or just a dialect of Welsh. And, while everybody had a theory, no one really knew what Pictish was.

Having, at least in broad strokes, placed the inscription's language in time and space, Vivian grabbed pen and notepad. Scanning the weathered letters again, she made a quick translation. Words she thought likely to be proper nouns were put into brackets while she offset confusing or unclear sections with parentheses.

The Great King [Tarkun] (causes to be raised?) this monument. (Unclear) house of the Great Counselor [Mirdin] in his honor. (Unclear) Great Counselor to King [Tarkun] for this (two-ten years?), formerly counselor to Great King [Arturus] of the sunset lands. With Great King [Tarkun's] blessings, [Mirdin] departs to the sunset lands to look upon (its?) green trees and endless water (one last time?).

The inscription was a potential bombshell. A career could be made, or broken, by those few lines in stone. But it might have implications far beyond that. A quick mental calculation told Vivian it was too early to call Uzbekistan. By the time she got home, made dinner, and settled in, it would be the perfect time to catch Dr. Grassley at camp before he left for the dig site.

Leftovers put away and coffee in hand, she sat at her computer. Dart, Vivian's black cat, orbited her legs, occasionally staring up at her with his yellow eyes and big ears. She thought about the scrawny kitten he'd been when he first appeared on her doorstep, one ear inexplicably smudged with motor oil.

Initiating a video chat, Vivian was rewarded with the image of Dr. Grassley's birdlike features, mop of white hair, and thick black-rimmed spectacles. "Dr. Cuinnsey, I thought I might be hearing from you."

"Dr. Grassley, what have you dug up?"

"It is a puzzle, isn't it, my dear? We're excavating near a small structure the locals venerate as the tomb of a Sufi saint. But we've dated it to the sixth century, a couple centuries too old for a Sufi." Grassley paused and cleaned his glasses. "Were you able to translate the Roman script on the stele? Was it Celtic?"

"It was. Common Brittonic, to be exact. And I was, most of it, anyway. I'm emailing the translation now. How did you know it was Celtic?"

"An educated guess. After making a phonetic transcription, I consulted the standard references and did some online research. Celtic was one of the few language families I couldn't rule out. So, I thought I'd see if you could shed any light on this little mystery."

"What are the other languages on the stele?" Vivian asked. "I didn't recognize either script."

"They are both in the Sogdian language," Grassley answered. "The first is the classical Sogdian script. The other is the slightly easier Manichean script. With the caveat that we understand rather less about Sogdian than Celtic, they both give translations broadly matching yours."

That pleased Vivian. Of course, it didn't really answer any questions about the stele or its inscriptions.

"Sogdian is distantly related to modern Farsi," he continued. "The spelling of this word 'Mirdin' on the stele is equivalent to 'Lord of God' or 'Noble of God.' I imagine this would translate conceptually as 'pious leader' or something like that, which sounds like a title. But notice that the word already accompanies the title 'Grand Vizier,' or what you translated as 'Great Counselor.' So, I am inclined to believe 'Mirdin' is a name, not a title."

Grassley flashed a mischievous smile. "Of course, 'Mirdin' would also be phonetically identical to the Celtic name of the individual commonly called Merlin, wouldn't it?"

"Careful, Grassley," Vivian shot back with hard-earned caution, "You're about to open one of the biggest cans of worms in Celtic studies. The historicity of Merlin, or Myrddin in Celtic, is very controversial. Even the affirmative camp posits Myrddin is an amalgam of multiple figures stretching across centuries. Arguing for the existence of a single individual analogous to the character from mythology is a good way to end a career."

"An intriguing point, given the reference to the 'Great King Arturus' and the 'sunset lands.'"

Thrilled by those same implications just hours ago, Vivian was suddenly in no mood to discuss them with the elderly archeologist. Again, she cautioned Dr. Grassley about the rabbit hole he was circling.

"You can grasp the momentousness of uncovering Latin inscriptions in Uzbekistan," he told her. "To say nothing of ones used to transliterate Celtic. We're holding a press conference about the discovery next week. I'd really like you to be here in Samarkand for it."

Vivian thought it over carefully. "I'm going to follow this development very closely. But, at this point, I can't justify taking time off from my department based on one find, no matter how unusual."

"Regrettable. I always enjoy seeing you. But I understand. I will keep you informed of any developments."

"One more thing, Grassley."

"Yes?"

"Not a word about the whole Merlin thing. Not one word."

Previews

Silver Screen Sleuths

"Red Hell, Green Murder"

Josh Reynolds

It was the worst heat wave the City of Angels had
experienced in almost forty years. The forty odd thousand
square foot confines of the interior jungle set for James
Whale's latest picture were almost as sweltering as the real
thing. The stage hands were in a war of attrition with the
humidity, and production assistants were waving clipboards
like fans, trying to keep the cast from melting. There were
rumours that Fairbanks had collapsed from heat stroke, and
that George Bancroft was running amok somewhere.

All in all, I was quite happy to be dead, and lounging in
the shade.

"About five of the worst pictures ever made are
crammed into this one," I said. I was on my third cigarette
of the morning. I held out the pack to Ray, who took one.

"The doctors say these will kill me," he said, before
lighting up. "And that's being a bit harsh, Vincent. We've
both been in worse films." He gave me a flat smile. "And
will be for many years to come, if the fates are kind."

"Speak for yourself," I said. "I suspect I've reached the
apex of my cinematic journey. Two poisoned arrows to the
chest and a bit of melodramatic writhing." I tapped my
chest for emphasis. "Hardly a praiseworthy career." It was
a bit part, but I got last billing. It's said that last billing is
better than no billing, but I was having a hard time seeing
the upside, career-wise. Such is the lot of the bit-player.

"Four years ago, I shared top billing with a horse and a dog," Ray said. "Now I'm playing a jungle savage, with fewer good lines than a character who got two poisoned arrows to the chest." He quirked an eyebrow and blew smoke at me.

"Don't forget the writhing. I am quite proud of the writhing."

"Almost Shakespearean."

"Well, I did get my start on the stage."

Ray laughed. There was nothing quite like watching Ray Mala laugh. His face, usually about as expressive as a chunk of teak, broke into canyons and crinkles. He clapped me on the shoulder, coughing slightly.

"That's why I like you, Vincent. You make me laugh."

"My talents are many and varied, Ray." I puffed on my cigarette and studied the interior of the subterranean Incan temple that had led to my most recent death. The studio had spared no expense on it—it rose wild, a blossom of heathen idolatry, crammed into a sound stage. It was the dais that drew the eye—a slab of faux-stone, surmounted by an immense menhir, ringed by a quartet of stylised, vaguely capric statues. Deer or goats or antelope, they didn't quite fit the theme. None of it did, really, despite the profuse amounts of plastic and paper flora clumped and scattered over the set in haphazard fashion.

Even so, it was a masterpiece far out of proportion with its current display. Cyclopean and intimidating, with an air of primitive mastery to it, it hinted at far better stories than the one currently playing out within it. I had no doubt Universal would use the set again, whenever they had need of something suitably exotic. Trade out the vines for sand, and it'd be a perfect Temple of the Seven Jackals or what have you.

"I heard Douglas tried to swing on one of the vines," Ray said. "Came off in his hand and dumped him on his ass."

188

"Serves him right. This isn't Zenda, and those aren't chandeliers."

"Did he swing on any chandeliers in that one?"

I blew a plume of smoke. "Not during the film."

Ray smiled. "You're just annoyed because he ran off with your wife."

I choked as smoke went down the wrong pipe. As I bent over, wheezing, Ray patted my back sympathetically. I knew he'd meant Joan Bennet, who played my late character's wife. My part was so miniscule that I hadn't had a chance to meet her before I was out, she was in, and the jungle was a-swelter with illicit romance between her character and Fairbanks' dashing adventurer. But for a moment—just an instant—I'd been thinking of Edi. My Edith.

Not unusual, all things considered. We'd been having some difficulties, of late. Broadway wasn't being kind to her, and none of the usual comforting pabulums were doing the trick. My successes, meagre though they were, weren't helping matters. Nor was the distance—she was still on the East Coast, while Hollywood had caught me up in its sun-drenched claws. I'd suggested we split the difference and move to Kansas, but she hadn't appreciated my attempt at humour. Edi was a tougher audience than Ray.

I forgot about Edi when the first scream echoed over the lot. Ray and I looked at one another. Then, a second scream followed the first, rising up like the wail of a fire engine. It was coming from the temple. We started forward, along with everyone else with two legs and a pair of ears. There was a stampede towards the looming eidolon, with its fake greenery and grisly decorations. One of the native girls—really, a former waitress from Long Island—stumbled into the open, eyes wide. She screamed again, showing off a set of lungs that would have made Weissmuller jealous.

Members of the crew were already crawling over the artificial edifice, seeking whatever it was that had set her to sounding the alarm. As we arrived, they found it.

Him, rather.

To the surprise of no one, shooting was cancelled for the rest of the day.

The next morning, I found myself in the scrap of a lot office that James Whale had claimed for his own. It was early enough that the drunks were singing in accompaniment with the birds on Cahuenga Boulevard, but the Universal backlot was silent. No scratch of tools or shouting teamsters. It was unnerving, I admit. You get used to the noise—the constant pressure of a hundred voices, all speaking at cross-purposes. It's only when it goes silent that you realise just how big and empty a sound stage truly is. An infinity of possibilities.

Whale looked like a man who'd been subsisting entirely on coffee and cigarettes for too long. He was still handsome, in that brittle British way, but you could see the cracks in the facade. The rumour was, he was on his way out. A shame, but then, I wasn't even *in*, so who was I to commiserate? Whale had been a name, once. A director on the rise.

But then the Laemmles had lost control in '36, when the studio went bankrupt. *Showboat* had sunk them, for all that it had been a success. And with the Carl and Junior out, Whale's rising star had turned into a falling one. I'd heard about the mess with the Germans and *The Road Back*— everyone in town had. Whale had won the battle, but lost the war. Rogers, the new studio head, was trying to figure out a way to get rid of him without breaking their contract, but Whale wasn't having any of it.

Thus, the great man had found himself directing a string of B-movies, including the currently in-production *Green Hell*. Whale was beaten down, with a hangdog look on his long, English features. Nonetheless, he eyed me keenly. "You made for an engaging Albert, when I saw you on stage a few years ago."

"It wasn't difficult. He was a charming man." I had played Prince Albert in the American production of Houseman's *Victoria Regina*. Not one of my more well-known roles, but one I was proud of, nonetheless.

Whale smiled. "Have you ever given thought to a more hardboiled part?"

"I'm open to opportunity," I said, trying to hide my eagerness. Was I being offered a part, in another film? My last starring role had involved being invisible for the majority of my screen-time. I don't recommend it.

The door closed behind me. I turned, and saw the familiar figure of the studio fixer, Earl Hoskins, looming in front of it. Imagine a chunk of granite, chopped carelessly, and stuffed into an expensive suit in an effort to hide the flaws in its shaping. That was Hoskins. Officially, he was just another studio executive. In reality, his purpose was more colorful than corporate. Hoskins was a new breed of middle man, designed and built by the studio system to make sure scandals stayed quiet, and that all the moving parts performed their function without interruption. "You ask him yet?"

"I was getting to it."

"Hurry up. I can't keep the cops off of the set forever."

"Then don't."

"This film is already over-budget and behind schedule." Hoskins spat the Four Deadly Words like bullets. Whale twitched but didn't otherwise react. I shrank slightly in my seat, trying to inch out of the line of fire.

Whale glanced at me. "You were on set yesterday? When they found it?"

"Yes. Poor Harold." I reached for the pack of cigarettes in my pocket. The body they'd found had been that of Harold Gummer. A security guard, and something of a fixture on the backlot. Elderly, even by the standards of Universal security guards. I hadn't known him well, but he'd seemed pleasant enough the few times we'd chatted. "Heart attack?"

"Arrows."

I stopped, the pack half out of my pocket. "Arrows?"

"Poison arrows. Just like the ones that did you in."

"But those are just props, surely?"

"Not when you break one in half and slide it between a guy's ribs," Hoskins grunted. He leaned against the door, arms crossed. "Better than a jailhouse shiv." The voice of experience, I assumed.

"The props department will be pleased to hear it." Whale looked at me. "It was murder. He was killed sometime the night before. The body was hidden."

I lit my cigarette. Given the heat, I was surprised someone hadn't stumbled over the body sooner, but I kept that little bon mot to myself. "Then why keep the police off the set?"

Hoskins set a heavy hand on my shoulder. "I thought you said he was smart?"

I glanced up at him. "This is about money?"

Hoskins grinned, despite my withering tone. "Look at that. He already found a clue."

Whale sighed. "The police will shut down the set. We're behind schedule already. But, if we can wrap things up nicely for them, before they start poking around, they might be inclined to accept our gift horse without first checking its teeth."

I sat back. "I'm starting to see where this is going. But why am I here?" I tensed. "Am I a suspect?"

"No. You'll be playing the detective." Whale tried to smile encouragingly. He didn't quite manage it.

"Why me?"

"You got a reason to be on set, even if you aren't doing anything. We hire a private dick, word gets out, the schedule goes to hell." Hoskins spoke flatly, grudging every word. He cracked his knuckles repeatedly, as if longing to thump someone.

"I know you're at loose ends, Vincent. I also know you're a good deal smarter than you pretend to be. You were an art procurer, for a brief time."

"Still am, in the slow months." When it came to buying art, it always helped to have a second pair of eyes. I was only too happy to provide those eyes, for a modest fee. Enough to cover the cost of a piece or two for my own collection.

"You have to have a good eye for forgeries in that line. The ability to see what a layman might miss. The little details."

I sat back, digesting this. As parts went, it wasn't the kind I'd had in mind. But, at the same time, I wasn't doing anything at the moment, being in something of a professional dry spell. And house rentals in the valley weren't cheap, on a bit player's income. Besides which, I'd liked Harold. No one ought to die on a film set. Not for real, anyway. I looked at Whale.

"I've always wanted to don the deerstalker. How much does it pay?"

"We're over budget," Hoskins growled.

"It will be worse, if the police get involved," Whale said, pointedly. He looked at me. "We'll bump your salary. You'll get what the leads are getting, in cash. Off the books." Behind me, Hoskins made a choking sound. Whale ignored him. "Does that sound fair?"

"More than adequate," I said. "I assume I am to begin by digging for suspects, among the cast and crew."

"I already know who did it," Whale said, bluntly. "I just need you to find them."

I stubbed out my cigarette in the ashtray on the table. "And who are they?"

"The Nazis," Whale said.

"It's not the Krauts," Hoskins said.

"I didn't say it was the Krauts," Whale said. "We've got

plenty of goose-stepping pricks here. Can't throw a rock in Illinois without hitting a Nazi." He leaned towards me, the shadows turning his face into a Greek tragedy mask. "Mark my words, Vincent—it's the Nazis. They hate my work. The only thing worse than a fascist is a critic."

"And the only thing worse than that is a critic who's a fascist," I said. Hoskins gave me the side-eye, and I quickly sheathed my rapier-like wit. I recovered quickly. "Why do you think it's the Nazis?"

"They've had it out for me since *The Road Back* premiered. You heard about it?"

"Who hasn't?" Whale's sequel to *All Quiet on the Western Front* had ruffled some feathers, including those of George Gyssling, the Los Angeles consul for the current German government. He'd squawked that the film had been unfair in its representation of the German people. Threats had followed, and the whole thing became one of those messes someone will inevitably write a book about, in a decade or two. "And you think they killed a security guard in order to shut down production?"

"I think there's nothing they wouldn't stoop to."

I leaned back, already in need of another cigarette. Instead, I nodded. Never argue with a director. A glance at Hoskins told me he felt the same. Whale's theory was unlikely, if only because he was no longer important enough to sabotage. At least not by the German government. But it was best to keep that to myself. I pushed myself to my feet.

"Even so, best to be thorough. I'll begin with the young woman who found the body, and go from there."

"You got a day, Price. That's all the budget allows for," Hoskins growled. "And I'll be watching to make sure you earn every penny."

"I feel more productive already. If you gentlemen will excuse me?"

As I left, another argument began. Or perhaps it was the

same one. Directors and producers were uneasy allies in the eternal war against rival studios, and Whale was harder to clamp down on than most.

Days like this, I was glad to be a humble thespian.

www.ingramcontent.com/pod-product-compliance
Lightning Source LLC
Chambersburg PA
CBHW060439180626
46817CB00007B/2894